WARD INVESTIGATION

SEAL's Pretend Girlfriend

SEAL's Pregnant Ex-Wife

SEAL's Fake Relationship

WARD INVESTIGATION : BOOK THREE

SEAL's Fake Relationship

USA TODAY BESTSELLING AUTHOR

LESLIE NORTH

BLURB

An old rivalry blooms into passion for a Navy SEAL and his fake girlfriend…

US Marshal Kelsey Poppins has an axe to grind. She's determined to prove her co-worker is innocent. But her old high school rival, Navy SEAL Ryan Ward, isn't convinced. His father died investigating a sinister crime ring. And he's convinced Kelsey's friend is involved…

But when they both sneak into a Federal building and find incriminating evidence within, her boss catches them in the act. Needing an excuse to explain his presence, Ryan leaves Kelsey weak-kneed with the *hottest* kiss she's ever had. Now, they're faking a relationship as they work together to solve a string of murders. All while trying to stay alive… And out of each other's arms.

Ryan won't allow one more person to die. Not on his watch, and definitely not Kelsey. Maybe it's the danger, the adrenaline rush of cheating death… But Ryan soon realizes he's falling for her, hard. And he's powerless to stop it.

When the investigation and their attraction both heat up, Ryan must decide what's more important. Catching the killers? Or keeping Kelsey safe…

MAILING LIST

Thank you for reading "SEAL's Fake Relationship"
(Ward Investigation Book Three)

Get SIX full-length novellas by USA Today best-selling author Leslie North for FREE! Over 548 pages of best-selling romance with a combined 3643 FIVE STAR REVIEWS!

Sign-up to her mailing list and get your FREE books:

www.leslienorthbooks.com/sign-up-for-free-books

CONTENTS

1

"Shooting down the walls of heartbreak…" Ryan Ward whispered before pulling the trigger.

Bang! Bang!

He glanced down the row at the paper target, two perfect holes straight through the center, and grinned, then tugged off his headphones.

"How the hell do you do that?" his brother Neal growled at him. All three brothers were sharing a single lane at the shooting range. It would have made more sense to line up separately so they wouldn't have to take turns—but then they couldn't mock and poke at each other while they were shooting which, obviously, was the most important part. "You're like the frigging Yoda of shooting or something," Neal said with a scowl. "You barely even looked at the target."

"When you've got it, you've got it," Ryan said with a smirk, stepping back to let Neal take his turn. "Not my fault I got all the sharpshooter genes while you got…hey, what *did* you get again?"

"'Gentlemen, you can't fight in here,'" their oldest brother, Lance, teased from behind them, quoting one of their favorite movies. "'This is the war room!' Or at least, a room with plenty of guns." Neal and Ryan just rolled their eyes. Ever since Lance had gotten back together with his ex-wife, who was pregnant with his child, he'd become a total goofball.

"So if we aren't going to fight, what are we supposed to do?" Neal asked, lining up his shot and then firing several times. "Hey, I know— we can talk about why Ryan's decided to leave his SEAL team."

"Nah, I think we should talk about how lousy your shooting has gotten. Think you might need glasses, bro?" Ryan examined the paper bullseye the machine had brought forward with mock concern. In truth, Neal was a good shot—all the Ward brothers were. But Ryan was the best. He never missed…except for metaphorically shooting himself in the foot.

It had been two and a half months since his final assignment with his SEAL team—since he'd charged in on a mission despite orders to stay put. It didn't matter that he hadn't been in the best headspace, having just learned his father had died. It didn't matter that his instincts had been *right,* and the mission would have failed without him. The navy had no use for a man who didn't follow orders. The best his CO could do was get him an honorable discharge, for mental health reasons.

Ryan snuck a look over at his two brothers, also former Navy SEALs. Neal had served with distinction until he'd been injured in the line of duty. Lance had put in twenty years with the navy and retired with full benefits. They were the best men he knew and he was proud to call them his brothers, but as the baby of the family, he'd spent his whole life trying to live up to their example. He wanted to wait a little longer before admitting to them just how badly he'd screwed up his military career. They could keep asking all they wanted—he would keep dodging their questions.

"Or maybe you just need some shooting lessons," Ryan suggested to Neal. "We could ask whoever's in that lane to our right—they're doing pretty well."

The person in there had been shooting since they got there, not saying a word, just firing and reloading and changing the bullseye, then starting again. Whoever they were, they had their headphones on and couldn't hear what the Ward brothers were saying anyway, so who cared. Ryan peered around the separator again at the anonymous shooter. At first, he thought it was a guy—on the short side, maybe half a foot shorter than Ryan's own six-foot-one. Slim, all dressed in black. Hair covered by a black ball cap and face obscured by the headphones and safety glasses and hat. Nothing that indicated gender one way or the other, but Ryan watched the person shoot, saw how they balanced against the recoil and realized it had to be a woman, based on the center of gravity.

His dad had been a private investigator and had taught Ryan plenty of tricks of the trade. Most especially trick number one: be observant. So he always had been. Sometimes, he'd use it as a party trick, showing off like Sherlock Holmes, but most of the time, he just quietly took note. The habit was so ingrained that he did it automatically. Without catching a glimpse of this person's face, he was already pretty sure he knew a number of things about her. She was practical, no frills. Highly trained, definitely not a civilian, but not military. Law enforcement of some sort would be his guess.

There was also something oddly familiar about the person...

Bang! Bang!

He returned to his own stall and watched Lance take his turn before sneaking a peek at his watch. They'd been here for a few hours now and he was ready for a beer. "Our time's about up," he announced. "How about we get out of here? Want to grab a drink at Swingin' Sue's? I'll buy first round."

He put his gear away, half-listening to his brothers talk about their love lives. Neal was focused on his upcoming wedding to their dad's old assistant, Lori. Lance couldn't shut up about Ruth and the baby they were expecting. And Ryan...well, Ryan had his new self-appointed mission. It wouldn't exactly keep him warm at night, but it would give him a sense of purpose again. And that, way more than any romance, was exactly what he needed.

On that topic, he actually did want to update his brothers on what he had in mind. "Hey, I think I found something interesting going over the intel from Dad's case earlier. Pretty sure there's a dirty US Marshal involved. It would explain a lot."

His words rang out in the suddenly silent shooting range. The woman in the next lane must have been reloading.

Lance stopped stuffing things in his duffle bag. "Seriously?"

"Yep." Their father's case had been a tangled mess from the start, but they were in the last stage of it now. They'd found the person who had killed their father, while trying to make it look like a natural death. They'd found the person who'd ordered the hit in the first place—the mob boss who'd been angry at Dad's investigation into one of his criminal rackets. But there was one piece of the puzzle still missing. "We know that Russo wanted Dad out of the way once he started looking into those prison inmate deaths. But we still don't know who got to those prisoners in the first place. For my money, it must have been a US Marshal."

"Wow," Neal said, blinking at Ryan. Then he cursed and turned away, brows knit. "It's an interesting idea. But you know Lori and I can't really help you look into it, right? We've got a full caseload on top of our wedding planning. That doesn't leave us with much time to spare to chase down some theory for you, bro, just based on your hunch."

It was more than a hunch, but Ryan let it slide. He got how busy Lori and Neal were, now that they were running Dad's PI business together. And he knew they'd already done their part for the overall investigation. It was Lori who had first chased down the idea that Dad had been murdered, working with Neal to find out who had done it. Then Lance and Ruth had followed the trail of the man who had ordered the hit. Lance and Neal and Lori and Ruth had all put a lot of time and effort into those cases.

When Ryan didn't answer, Neal went on. "But I get the appeal of wanting to solve the final piece of the puzzle for Dad's last case. Especially since the trail's gone cold and the police have given up on it."

"Does anyone else think the Marshals are involved?" Lance asked, frowning.

Ryan took a deep breath and shook his head. "Nope. Just me, for now."

"Hmm." Lance picked at the front of his jacket. "And closing this case is really what you think you should be doing right now? Instead of going back to your SEAL team?"

Going back to his SEAL team wasn't an option, not that Lance knew that. All he'd told his brothers was that he'd decided to leave the military so he could focus on finishing this case. If they happened to assume that he'd *voluntarily* left the navy to work this investigation, that wasn't his fault. He hadn't actually said that—even if he'd maybe implied it, hoping to stop the questions about how he could still be on bereavement leave weeks after any real leave would have ended.

"Of course," Ryan said. This wasn't an avoidance tactic. He really did want to find out that last person responsible for their dad's death. Maybe then his grief would finally lessen over that whole thing, because damn. His chest still ached over it. Too much loss too close together. First Dad, then his SEAL team… He brushed it off, staring down at the graffiti-carved tabletop. "It's what's best for me."

Liar.

Lance paused a beat or two, then nodded, his expression unreadable as he finished securing his gun case and picked it up. "Because going down a rabbit hole trying to arrest every criminal in the city who's even tangentially related to Dad's death isn't what he would've wanted for you."

"I know that. I'm not an idiot, bro." His shoulders tensed, the muscles in his upper back knotting tight with frustration. Yes, he had other shit, important shit, going on, but that wasn't what was happening here. It wasn't. He wasn't avoiding what had happened. He was just letting it sit a bit, digest, then he'd deal with it all when the time came. There was the sound of shuffling feet from the stall on his other side, then a couple of clicks as the person reloaded. Still shooting away without a care in the world. *Lucky.* "Look, guys. I'm fine, okay? If neither of you wants to be involved in my investigation of the marshals, I'll do it myself. But for the record? It's not a wild goose chase. I've got a plan."

"Oh, Jesus." Neal shook his head, chuckling. "Not another plan."

"Right?" Lance said, laughing. "We've been down that road too many times with you, little bro."

Ryan flipped them both off, then sat forward, lowering his voice to avoid being heard in the quieter place. "Seriously. Just hear me out. I want to sneak into the local US Marshal's office to get a look at some files and—"

"And?" a voice said beside him, cutting him off. "Please go on describing how you plan to break into a law enforcement facility. That sounds like a really excellent idea to discuss, especially in public. No wonder your friends don't seem impressed by your planning skills."

He froze. That voice. He knew that voice. His heart sank as the woman from the next lane pulled off her hat to reveal long red hair and a face he knew all too well. His old high school nemesis, Kelsey Poppins.

Oh shit.

"And the best part of the plan was definitely to bring it up in front of a US Marshal." Kelsey was watching him with a superior look. Perfect. Just great. Same old rivalry, still alive and well. Same little tingle of awareness inside him too. Shit. Even worse, she was a US Marshal now. He might have seen that on her social media profiles earlier. Not that he'd been looking. Nope. Okay, time to redirect the conversation.

"Kelsey, good to see you," he said. "I don't think you know my brothers—let me introduce you." He stretched out the introductions as long as he could, hoping to get her engaged in some other topic so that she'd let drop what she'd overheard…but he should have known better than to think that would work. Kelsey had always been like a dog with a bone. Once she latched on to something, she never let go.

"So this plan of yours to break into the office—" she began. "You know I'll have to report you, right?"

"Report what?" he asked. "Report that you *thought* you heard me making a joke with my brothers in a gun range?"

"I know what I heard," she answered, undeterred. "And you weren't joking."

No, he wasn't, but he wouldn't admit that to her. Not yet. Because come to think of it, this could be a great opportunity. If he could get her to help him, it would make it ten times easier to get into the office and get access to the files he needed. But she wouldn't agree easily, so he'd have to…*guide* her to the decision.

"Wasn't I? Can you really be sure? It's noisy here, and you were wearing headphones most of the time we were talking. Plus, you were pretty distracted for a while there, weren't you? Rough day at work, so you came here to blow off some steam…only you weren't hitting the targets like you wanted to, and that just made it worse, right?" He'd heard the way she'd tsked and huffed at herself over shots that didn't land quite right. Her aim had smoothed out the longer she'd stayed, but she'd seemed pretty frustrated at the start, which hinted that it hadn't been a good day overall.

"I was hitting the targets just fine!" she said, face flushed bright red. So she was still just as bad a liar as she'd been in high school. It was a little endearing. "Better than *you* could do, I'm sure."

Gotcha.

"Better than me? Are you sure?" he asked, using his skeptical tone to bait her as much as possible.

"Of course I'm sure!"

"Then you wouldn't mind making a little wager?"

"I…what?"

"A shooting competition. Right here, right now. Two shots. Best bullseye wins. If I win, you have to sneak me into your offices to see the files I want."

"I *knew* you weren't joking about wanting to get in!"

"Maybe I was, maybe I wasn't. It only matters if I win, though. If *you* win, I promise I'll drop my idea completely. So do we have a deal? Or are you not so sure of your shooting skills after all?" He watched her closely, waiting to see what she'd decide. The Kelsey Poppins he remembered always rose to a challenge. Was that part of her still the same?

Kelsey straightened and gave him a curt nod. "Fine. Let's do it."

"Okay." He couldn't help grinning as he winked at his brothers, who stood behind him shaking their heads, then got his stuff out again. Both he and Kelsey got locked and loaded, put up new targets at the end of their lanes, then waited.

"Ladies first," he said, waiting as she took her stance and fired.

Bang! Bang!

She pressed the button to bring her target back to her, staring at him the whole time with a defiant grin. And fuck it all, it turned him on. He pushed that thought away and locked it down. He was on a mission here—and he would never let anything distract him from that. He turned his attention to her paper target. Not bad. Two holes pierced the center. Not quite exact middle, but darned close.

"Nicely done," he said as he slammed a full magazine into his Glock. "But now it's my turn."

Then Ryan turned and fired two shots.

Bang! Bang!

Ryan pressed his button, his gaze on Kelsey the entire time as the machine slowly churned and the paper target rustled forward on its hook and chain.

"Jesus Christ," Neal said again. "How the hell do you do that?"

Ryan grinned from ear to ear, taking the target down without looking at it and handing it to Kelsey. When her gaze flicked down to it, the pretty pink color drained from her cheeks.

"Fuck," she said, just confirming what he'd already known. He'd won.

Only one hole sat dead center in the target, because both bullets had passed through it cleanly.

"You…you win," she admitted, sounding so gutted by the fact that Ryan felt a pang of remorse. Had it been a jerk move to manipulate her into this situation? He could get tunnel vision when he was on a mission, so focused on the end goal that he didn't pay attention to what he was screwing up along the way.

"It was a dumb bet," he said, words spilling out in an unpracticed rush. "We can forget about it."

Her eyes flew up to meet his, and whatever she saw on his face actually made her soften a bit. "A deal's a deal," she said. "And you won the bet."

"Tell you what," he offered, "why don't you come over to Swingin' Sue's with us? We can tell you some more about the situation. When I'm done, if you still think I'm totally off base, you'll have your chance to try to change my mind. Sound fair?"

"Yeah," she agreed. "Sounds fair."

Fifteen minutes later, they walked into the bar across the way. The place was about forty years old and the interior looked it, faded paint and water-stained ceiling. But the drinks were cheap, and the food was good. Plus, the owner had been a friend of their dad's, so it kind of felt like a home away from home.

Lance held up four fingers toward the bartender to get them their beers, and they took a seat at a booth near the back. Neal and Lance took one side of the booth, leaving Ryan and Kelsey to share the other. Once the server brought their drinks and departed, Ryan took a swig of beer, then got down to business. "Kelsey, my brothers and I have been looking into what happened to our father ever since his funeral. I'm sure you've heard on the news that he was murdered. We helped catch the killer and the mob guy who ordered the hit."

She nodded, staring down at her bottle. "Yeah, I saw."

"Well, there's still one more piece to solve. The part they aren't really talking about on TV is why our dad was looking into the mob in the first place. Dad was hired by a local lawyer—" Lance's ex-wife, Ruth, "—because some of the clients she represented were dying very suddenly of heart attacks in jail. And it always happened right after changing their pleas to guilty for crimes she was very sure they didn't commit. When the mob realized my dad was looking into it, *he* suddenly died of a supposed heart attack, too. Over the past two and a half months, we've uncovered everything that happened, except for one thing—who actually killed the prisoners? It couldn't be a prison guard because the killer would have to have access to multiple different prisons. Unlikely that it was a prisoner, or even a group of prisoners who were with the mob, because most of the guys died in their cells and didn't have mob-affiliated cellmates. A police officer would have no excuse for visiting all of those prisoners, so it would draw too much attention. Also, nearly all of the prisoners with suspicious deaths died on a day when they were transported. And since prisoner transport is handled by the US Marshals, well..." He shrugged. "That makes them the most likely candidates in my book. If I can look at the records to see who handled transport of those prisoners on those days, I'll be able to see if there's a pattern."

"There isn't," she said, sounding absolutely certain. "No US Marshal would do anything like that."

"Then I'll see the paperwork, realize there's no pattern after all and have to come up with a new theory."

She opened her mouth, as if she wanted to say something else, but then shut it, still thinking. Finally, she spoke. "Those files are confidential." Her auburn brows drew together as she glanced first at him, then his brothers, then back to him again, her expression worried. "I could get in a lot of trouble if I'm caught. I could lose my job."

Damn. If there was one thing she could have said to get him to cave, it would be that. He was already going through the pain of losing the career he loved, and he wouldn't wish it on anyone.

Ryan sighed. "Look. I'm not trying to get you fired or in trouble, Kelsey. If you think there's another way I can get a look at that information, then tell me and I'll try that instead."

She seemed to consider that a moment, then shook her head, her expression unreadable. "No. We'll do it your way. I'll get you the files. Then you'll see that I'm right and it wasn't a US Marshal after all. But," she held up a finger. "It's on my terms and my rules. I can't let you wander all over by yourself. Understand?"

He nodded, just glad it was still on.

"Good." She took a long swig of beer, wiping her mouth on the back of her hand. "We can work out the details tomorrow."

2

"No," Kelsey said the next morning as she and Ryan sat across from each other at a little coffee shop near her office. It was where they'd agreed to meet so they could plan out how they'd get Ryan in to see the files he needed. "That won't work at all. We need to keep it simple and stay cautious."

Of course, the words "simple" and most especially "cautious" had never been in the same sentence as Ryan Ward, so they disagreed. About literally everything. As always. Jesus H. Christ. It was like she'd stepped back in time ten years and they were in high school again, bickering over anything and everything while he teased her and pranked her every chance he got. He had always been the most frustrating, aggravating, infuriating, gorgeous…wait, no, that last part was something she wasn't supposed to think about. He might be movie-star handsome—even more so now than in high school, his body having filled out in all the best ways in the nine years since they'd graduated—but that didn't change the fact that "trouble" was practically his middle name.

"No," he said, frowning and sitting back in his chair, his long legs tangling with hers under the table. She compressed her lips and avoided kicking him. Barely. "It's not enough for you to get the files and then just show them to me later. I want to be there with you. Talk to people." At her "are you serious" look, he waved her off. Overconfident to a fault. Same shit, different day. "Don't worry. I'll come up with a cover. I'm good at that. It's what I'm trained to do."

Uh-huh.

Kelsey rolled her eyes, then shook her head. "Look, I get that you're a SEAL, Ryan. That's a big deal. Congratulations. This isn't an undercover mission where you've got a whole team behind you, making sure everything goes according to plan. This is just us—and if we mess it up, I'd lose a job that I really love. There's no reason for you to be in my office, Ryan. You said you wanted the files, and I can get them and share them with you electronically. That way you can see if there are any suspicious patterns. Easy-peasy. No personal contact necessary."

He scoffed and straightened. "Checking the files is only the beginning. The real detective work comes from talking to people and following any leads as they pop up. I do my best work face to face. I need to see things, touch things, assess the details."

Yeah, I bet you do.

She bit back the words before they got out. She should have expected this. He'd always been cocky as hell. She'd hoped that military service might ground him a little, but she supposed that was asking too much. His ego was so bulletproof, it couldn't be punctured by a ballistic missile. He'd always been too smooth and good-looking for his own good. Charming the pants off everyone to get exactly what he wanted. Well, not this time, buddy. And yes, maybe she'd had a little crush on him back then. Fine. A huge crush. Didn't mean any of that transferred over to now. Nope.

She continued to press her point. "I'm telling you it won't work. This is where I work every day, Ryan. I know these people. I know this process. You waltzing in there, pretending to be some hot-shot with whatever cover you make up, will only piss people off." She crossed her arms and glared at him. For once, why the hell couldn't he admit that she knew best? It felt like he was completely discounting her professional expertise. Always the same story with him. He knew best, so he was in charge and everyone else were his minions. "I'm not going to let you use this as some chance to show off. You're not going to find anything anyway, so just let me handle it."

"Show off, huh? Is that what you think this is about?" He leaned forward, close enough for her to see the tiny gold flecks in his green eyes beneath his long dark lashes. She'd have killed for those damned lashes instead of the pale reddish-blonde ones that went with her red hair and freckles. "Look, I know I messed around a lot in high school, but believe me, showing off is the last thing on my mind right now. Do you have any idea how important this case is to me? How personal it is? This is my dad we're talking about here."

Kelsey's heart twinged sympathetically. She had always been close with her parents, so she could relate. But still… "You and your brothers caught the man who killed him. And you caught the man who ordered the murder. This last person, whoever it is, was involved in the crime ring, yes, but he or she had nothing to do with your dad, personally."

"But they're part of the case," Ryan answered, his jaw set. "My dad was a great investigator. He never left a case unfinished. This was his last case—the final thing he worked on, the thing he *died* working on. I can't turn back the clock and save him, no matter how much I wish I could. The last thing I can do for him is see it through."

Dammit. Her face felt hotter than the surface of the sun. Another redhead curse—easy blushing. He had to go and play that card, getting her to care. She'd been hoping she could just give him the files, show him he was wrong about her fellow marshals, and they could go their separate ways. But now she was starting to get interested in the case. After everything he had been through, he deserved to be able to complete the investigation, to get that closure that he so clearly needed. On the other hand… "Look, I get where you're coming from," she said. "I understand why this is so important to you. But that just makes it all the more important to do this right. You want answers, right? I want them for you, too. And I have five years of experience working in that office and know how it runs. So maybe you should try actually *listening to me* when I say what's going to help you get the info you need, and what's going to end up with you getting thrown out of the office with no answers at all."

He opened his mouth to reply but was interrupted by the server stopping by to refill their coffees and leave the check.

By the time the waitress left, they were back to staring at each other across the table, a silent stand-off. Same old, same old. Always the same with them. From day one back in high school they'd been rivals. Kelsey was never sure exactly why, except that they were polar opposites in just about every way. And the fact they'd been stuck together in nearly all their classes. For some reason, Ryan had been her greatest competition. Battling for the best grades, fighting for the teacher's attention. He'd matched her step for step and she'd found it infuriating. He was always there. Always in her face. Always seemed to be studying her, watching her, like she was some kind of science experiment. She'd never asked him why. Didn't want anything to do with him, really. He'd taken up too much real estate in her head back then as it was. Precious space she'd needed for studying if she was going to get into college on a full scholarship like she'd planned. Never mind if he was cute and funny and sexy as hell. She didn't care about any of that. Nope. Not at all. Ryan Ward was the last man on earth she'd ever be interested in that way. Period. Amen. Thank you very much for playing.

Seconds turned into minutes and neither one of them blinked, until finally he groaned and let his head fall back until he was staring at the ceiling. Kelsey bit back a grin.

Ding, ding, ding. We have a winner.

"Ugh. Fine. We'll do it your way." He cursed under his breath and shook his head, gulping down more coffee, then hissing. "But I still want to be there. You mentioned earlier that your coworkers were going out to lunch for someone's retirement party today, yeah? We can go in then. I'll check the transport files, and then I'll leave."

Kelsey still would have preferred to keep him out of the office alto-gether—but this was probably the best compromise she was going to be able to get. And he was right about the timing. With her co-workers gone, it would be the best time to get the files. And since no one else would be there, he couldn't schmooze anyone else in her office and piss them off. She stood and grabbed the check. "Fine. Let's go."

After they paid, he followed her out of the coffee shop and across the parking lot to the nondescript office building adjacent to the strip mall. There was nothing really to differentiate it from the dentist's offices and medical clinics around the area, other than the sign out front near the curb with the US Marshals logo emblazoned on the wood. They tried to keep things low-key. It wasn't a flashy job but it was an important one.

She'd made some excuse earlier about having to miss the retirement party to catch up on some paperwork at the office, so she and Ryan window shopped a bit in front of a discount department store, waiting for her coworkers to leave. They were more than happy for Kelsey to stay behind in case of an emergency.

Once the coast was clear, she led him to the rear entrance of the building, the one not monitored by security cameras, and unlocked the door to let him inside. Her desk was near the back corner of the office and she dropped her keys off there before logging into her computer and pulling up the files he'd requested to see.

Ryan propped his hip on her desk beside her and leaned in, his heat and nearness making her more aware of him than she wanted to be. He smelled obnoxiously good. Kelsey logged in, then did a search in the records for the prisoner names he'd given her to see who was assigned to their transportation. The files pulled up one by one and she printed out the pages they needed—the ones for the days when each of the prisoners had died.

"Here we go," she said, when they had all the pages printed and spread out on her desk.

"Cool." Ryan leaned closer, his breath stirring the hair at her temple, and Kelsey suppressed a shudder. Where the hell had that come from? It was just nerves, that was all. She was afraid one of her coworkers might have forgotten something and would come back in to get it, catching them. Yep. That was it.

"Well, well, well," Ryan said after a moment, and it took her a second to connect the dots of what he was talking about. "Looks like we've got ourselves a dirty Marshal. Two of them, actually."

"What?" Kelsey frowned at the names he was pointing at. Phil Johnson and Kenny Burk. She didn't know Kenny all that well—he'd transferred out of their offices earlier in the year and prior to that, he'd mostly kept to himself—but Phil was her boss. She didn't want to believe it could be true, that he could be involved in some kind of criminal conspiracy, but sure as hell, their names were on nearly every one of the transport files where the prisoner ended up dead. "Dammit."

"Guess my theory wasn't so crazy after all," Ryan said softly. If he'd sounded cocky or smug, she might have smacked him, but his tone seemed almost sympathetic, as if he knew how upsetting this was for her.

"Maybe there's another explanation," she said, her voice almost pleading. "There's one case where it *wasn't* them on transport, see?"

"Yeah, but the same name on *all* the rest? That can't be a coincidence. My guess? They were able to shuffle schedules on the rest of them to make sure they got the assignment to transport each of these prisoners —but with that last one, they couldn't make it work, so one or both of them came up with a reason to visit the prison and handle the job later that day," Ryan said.

She couldn't quite handle the thought of meeting his eyes, so she got busy printing out the rest of the files for the inmates. They would need all the info they could get in order to prove what the two marshals had done. The last thing she wanted to do was keep working with Ryan Ward on this, but there really wasn't another choice now, considering that she'd seen evidence of wrongdoing with her own eyes. If there was one thing Kelsey couldn't stand, it was wrongdoing. The motto of the US Marshals was "Justice, Integrity, Service." She was going to make sure they lived up to that.

"Move," she said, when she got back to her desk from the printer, jabbing Ryan with her elbow so he slid off her desk. "We need to look into these files more to make sure we've got all the evidence we need to nail these assholes."

He frowned. "Uh, wait a minute. That sounds like you're going to keep helping me."

"Damn straight, I am." She gave him a look. "I don't want corrupt marshals screwing things up for the rest of us."

"I'm not sure that's a good idea." He frowned. "This would mean digging into your coworkers—people you've known and worked with for years. Do you really think you can handle that?"

She bristled. "Of course I can. Are you saying I can't?"

Unfortunately, he never got to answer because the sound of the keypad beeping at the front entrance had them both tensing up.

"Shit!" Kelsey said, shoving the printouts into her desk drawer. "Get in the supply closet. Hurry!"

"Uh, I've got a better idea," Ryan said, grabbing her around the waist and pulling her to him. Kelsey was honestly too stunned to do anything but blink up at him. "Trust me."

Before she could ask what he was talking about, his mouth was on hers and they were kissing.

3

———————

The door opened and Ryan kept his lips pressed to Kelsey's, holding her body close and trying to make it look as convincing as possible. He had one hand on her lower back, the other tangled in her hair. Her ponytail had come loose and now all that red silk spilled through his fingers. She sighed, her stiff posture going lax against him, and suddenly it didn't feel so pretend anymore. Distracted, he pressed a little hard, opening her lips to his tongue, which he dipped inside to taste her. Coffee and hazelnut creamer and sweetness. Delicious. If it wasn't for the rude question yelled from behind them, he could have continued on like that for a while.

"What the hell is going on here?" a loud male voice demanded.

Reluctantly, Ryan ended the kiss, pulling back slightly to notice Kelsey's slightly dazed expression. Wrong or not, pure male satisfaction swelled inside him. He'd made her look like that. Certain parts of his body cried out for him to do it again.

Mustering all his willpower, he ignored those body parts and took a deep breath to steady himself before turning around to face the asshole who'd interrupted them. It was going to be up to him to handle this, he knew. Kelsey was a horrible liar, always had been. If they were going to sell this story, he'd have to be the one doing the selling. "What? It's against the law now to kiss your girlfriend?"

The guy who'd barged in on them looked surprised. But he had nothing on Kelsey, who'd snapped out of her post-kiss haze at his last word.

"Girlfriend?" she said at the same time the mystery man did.

If he hadn't been in deep shit here, Ryan would have laughed. Was it really that hard to believe that he and Kelsey would be dating? He looked back at her in her buttoned-up, prim-looking suit and sensible shoes. Sure, she wasn't his standard type—but this guy didn't know him, didn't know what he looked for in the fun hookups that were his usual MO. If he was looking for a girlfriend—an actual, serious commitment—why *wouldn't* he want someone like Kelsey? She wasn't flashy, but she was beautiful, smart, passionate, and she kissed like…

He started to lean in again but stopped himself. *Whoa there, cowboy.*

They weren't here to make out, no matter how enjoyable that might be. They were here to work on his dad's case. The sooner he focused on that, the better. Turning to Kelsey, he mustered up a rueful smile. "You didn't tell the people you work with about me, sweetheart?"

"Uh." Pretty pink color rose in her cheeks and he found himself fascinated by it until he blinked hard.

"Oh well, I guess I can understand that," Ryan said smoothly, jumping into the cover story that he was already forming in his head. "There wouldn't have been much point while we were doing the long-distance thing, right? But now that I'm here to stay, there's no reason to keep it to ourselves. I know you like to keep your work and your personal life separate, but it's like I've been telling you, baby—your friends are going to be nothing but happy for us." Ryan turned to the man, giving him a warm smile. "Hey there, I'm Ryan Ward—Kelsey's boyfriend." He held his hand out for a shake.

Eyeing him warily, the man took it. "Phil Johnson," he said—and it took everything Ryan had not to react to one of the names he and Kelsey had just flagged. "Nice to meet you, Ryan."

"Thanks. Same." They shook, then Ryan slid his arm around Kelsey's waist before she could get away from him. She stood stiffly beside him. "Nice office you have here, sir."

"Hmm." Phil gave them both a wary look. Ryan wasn't sure if he was suspicious of their act or if he just really hated PDAs. Either way, Ryan made sure to maintain steady eye contact, no hint of hesitation, like he had nothing to hide. Just like Dad had taught him. "Yes, it is nice. But there are certain behaviors that are not very workplace appropriate. In the future, Kelsey, please try to keep that in mind."

"Yes, sir. Of course," Kelsey said, looking mortified and flustered, her face hot enough now that Ryan could feel it. "I'll, uh, just walk Ryan out to his car, then."

Phil watched him, his expression disapproving as they headed for the door. Once they were alone out in the parking lot, Kelsey rounded on him. "What the actual fuck was that back there?"

Ryan took a step back, holding up his hands, his tone as conciliatory as he could make it. "Look, we were going to get caught anyway. And you were going to get flustered and start stammering because you've never been able to lie your way out of a paper bag." She squawked at that, and he just waited, knowing she couldn't actually argue the point. After a minute, she grumbled something and nodded, so he continued. "Anyway, if you were going to act embarrassed and like you had something to hide, we needed to give you a reason for it *other* than sneaking someone in to look at confidential documents. Getting embarrassed over getting caught with your boyfriend seemed like it would fit the bill. Plus, now that they think we're dating, it won't be weird for me to spend more time around you. I can pick you up at the office or whatever and no one will think twice about it. No suspicions at all. Not even your corrupt boss back there."

Kelsey looked totally unconvinced. "No one's going to believe we're actually together."

"Hey, it worked for my brother Neal and his fiancée Lori when they were investigating Dad's case. Now they're together for real." When he realized what he'd said there at the end, he frowned and cleared his throat. "Not that that would happen with us. Nope."

She crossed her arms and narrowed her gaze. "How the hell am I supposed to keep up this whole fake relationship façade, then, without giving it away by being a bad liar?"

"That's the beauty of it, though." He smiled. "Keep doing the whole blushing, stammering, awkwardness thing and people will just assume you're self-conscious about our relationship, not that you're lying about it in the first place."

Kelsey watched him for a long moment, then sighed. "Fine. I guess it makes a sort of twisted sense." She glanced back at the office, then to him again. "So, what's our next step? We still need to go over these printouts more closely."

"Yep." He took out his phone. "What's your number?"

She rattled it off to him and Ryan typed it into his contacts, then sent her a text. "I sent you my dad's old address. It's where I'm staying right now. Come over tonight around seven and we can start investigating things."

～

After Ryan left, Kelsey came back inside and sat down at her desk. She'd hoped that Phil would have gotten whatever he'd come back to the office for and then returned to the retirement lunch thing, but no. Phil stayed there and even called Kelsey over to his desk. Her stomach dropped a little as she walked over and caught a glimpse of his screen, where he'd pulled up her computer activity—something he had access to as her supervisor. So he knew she'd pulled up the files about the prisoner transfers.

Shit.

"Kelsey," Phil said, scowling at his screen, then her. "Want to tell me exactly what you were looking for in these digital files? They're not part of your current caseload."

"I, uh…" *Think, dumbass.* Panic rose within her as it always did when she had to lie. She hated it. Her throat started to constrict as she blurted out the first excuse she could think of. "I was just making sure that the older files would still load, since my computer updated to the new operating system this morning. Everything worked fine, by the way."

Oh God. Everything was definitely not fine. Inside, she was a mess. Palms sweaty, heart thundering, the rush of blood in her ears so loud it nearly drowned out all else. She swallowed hard past her constricted throat and stared at her computer screen, cheeks hot as the weight of Phil's stare prickled her skin. Honestly, she could have been so much farther along in her career if she could lie—even white lies and flattery to her superiors. Her coworkers did it all the time, and got promotions and plum assignments and cases that gained them lots of praise and publicity. But Kelsey just couldn't.

She sucked at it. Ryan was right.

Ryan.

Why did he have to kiss her? She would have been perfectly content to just work the case with him and keep things perfectly professional, but now that wasn't an option. He'd kissed her and she'd never be able to forget it. Even if she knew nothing could come of it. History had taught her well. Once a guy she liked saw her whole self, her true self, he couldn't handle it. It had happened to her time and time again. The first time was back in high school when she'd had a crush on a popular jock. He'd been interested too, at least until she'd beaten him at basketball during a silly spirit week event. After that, he'd changed his mind about taking her to prom. Or college, when she and her boyfriend had gone from discussing marriage to going their separate ways after she'd told him she didn't want kids. Then there was the short-lived romance with a fellow marshal right out of training. That one had ended because they didn't have anything in common outside the job. Finally, there was the most recent and most painful one. John. The banker. They'd met on a dating app and had wanted all of the same things in life—security, love, faithfulness, fun, companionship, passion. They'd gone out for nine months, but the longer they were together, the more frustrated John had gotten with Kelsey's work schedule. Being a US Marshal wasn't exactly a typical nine-to-five job. She'd had to travel a lot. Her work put her in danger sometimes. John didn't like any of that.

But the tipping point for them had come after they got mugged one night after leaving a restaurant downtown. Kelsey had defended them against the mugger. Another passerby had recorded it all on their phone and posted it online. She'd thought John would be proud of how capable she was, but no. He'd been embarrassed and ashamed that his girlfriend had taken the mugger down, not him. Said he'd gotten teased endlessly by his coworkers because of it. That, coupled with all John's other insecurities about their relationship, had brought things to a swift and brutal conclusion shortly thereafter.

So yeah. She refused to put herself through that again. It just wasn't possible to find someone who accepted all of her. And she knew better than to think that Ryan would be the exception. As far as she could tell, he found *all* of her annoying. Nope. She wasn't touching that with a ten-foot pole.

Even if the angels do sing in my head when he kisses me.

Flustered and frustrated, Kelsey hazarded a glance up at her boss and found Phil looking at her like she was something gross he'd stepped in that was now smeared on the bottom of his shoe. They'd never really gotten along. She suspected Phil tolerated her because she was good at her job and made him look good as a consequence. When she still didn't move after a long beat, he said dismissively, "You can go."

"Right. Thank you." *Why the hell am I thanking him? He's a dick! Stop talking, Kelsey.*

She stood, discombobulated and annoyed at herself. She was a good Marshal. She'd worked hard to get where she was, and to have Phil act like such an ass pissed her off even if she was used to it. It was just one more thing on a day that had thrown her for a loop. But for all that she didn't much like him, she still didn't want to believe that he could be dirty, no matter what the evidence said. She thought back to the files she and Ryan had pulled—to the one inmate who had died on a day when Phil and Kenny hadn't, officially, been anywhere near him. Was Ryan right? Had the men gone to the prison to handle the job there? But wait, if she was remembering the dates correctly, then Phil couldn't have done it, because—

"I was…um…thinking of taking a vacation sometime soon and I… uh…w-wanted to ask you about that trip you took to Vermont last year to see the foliage," she managed to force out. "It was nice, right? And, um, when were you there? W-was it around October 19th? Am I remembering that right?"

He raised his eyebrows and gave her a withering look, but then clicked open his electronic calendar. "Yes, I was in Vermont from October 15 to 22. And yes, it was quite nice. Will that be all?"

"Y-yes, sir," she said before retreating to her desk posthaste.

She knew she'd probably sounded like an idiot, but at least she'd been able to get the information she needed. She remembered Phil going on that trip. And now that she knew those dates meant he was definitely out of town for one of the murders, she felt a weight lift off her shoulders. She might not like the man, but she hadn't looked forward to busting her boss for murder. Must have been all Kenny Burk doing the mob's dirty work.

When she went to meet Ryan that night, she told him about Phil's vacation right away.

Ryan did not seem as happy as she'd expected. "Okay, first of all, why the hell did you ask him about his whereabouts? That would just make him suspicious."

"No, it wasn't like that," she insisted. "I didn't ask him anything about the prisoners or about transport. I just said I was thinking of taking a vacation and asked what the foliage was like in Vermont in October. It's fine—he doesn't know it's connected to anything else."

"Hmm," Ryan said, looking unconvinced. "If he *was* guilty, then you would have given us away. But if he really wasn't in town, then I guess you got lucky and he's not our guy. We'll shift our focus to Kenny Burk for now. On paper his career is solid but undistinguished, giving him the obvious advantage of flying under the radar." He rifled through Kenny's file on the table. "And it looks like he took a leave of absence to go through a department-mandated rehab program for alcohol. Huh. If he had issues with addiction, that might have been how the mob got to him. Maybe he was into more than just alcohol."

"You're thinking drugs?"

Ryan shrugged. "Could be. It's not uncommon to have multiple addictions. Once the mob had him, they could blackmail or bribe him to cooperate. When he got back on the job, clean and sober, is when he asked to move to undercover work. Interesting."

"I think the next thing we do is go to Internal Affairs once we've found those files from the printout," she said. "Do it all by the book."

But Ryan was already shaking his head. "No. We need to build more of a case first for them to take us seriously."

Kelsey wanted to argue, but she was uncomfortably aware that he had a point. While she'd love to just hand the whole mess over to IA, they didn't have enough evidence yet. They'd have to keep working together a while longer. "Fine. So let's start tracking down Kenny Burk first. Figure out if he's still working for the US Marshals or not and if he's not, then where he's employed now."

"Okay." Ryan led her over to the sofa where they took a seat, and Kelsey spread out the printouts from earlier on the coffee table. Ryan picked up several and studied them. "Well, according to these, the last time Burk worked on a prisoner transport was about nine months ago, right before my dad's death. If we can track him down, we can figure out if we can tie him to the murder when Burk wasn't handling the transport."

4

———————

The next day, Ryan and Kelsey went downtown to visit the US Marshals Personnel office in the Patrick V. McNamara Federal Building. They'd worked out a plausible story the night before at Ryan's place, and they'd agreed that Ryan would do most of the talking. Hopefully their story would hold up, and Kelsey wouldn't blow it because of her issues with lying. Ryan crossed his fingers anyway.

Ding. The elevator doors slid open and they weaved through the other people in the car to get off. Kelsey straightened her suit jacket and headed down the hall to the Marshals' office without waiting to see if he followed. Ryan shook his head and trailed after her. They'd seemed to be getting along pretty well the previous night, going through the files and making a plan together, but it was like every time they separated, she'd spend the hours reminding herself that she didn't like him, and a wall would be back up between them the next time they met. His brothers would say that he just didn't know what to do with someone he couldn't charm, but the truth was, the way she seemed to think that the world would end if she ever even considered letting her guard down around him hurt his feelings a little. Back in high school, when they'd competed over anything and everything, he'd always enjoyed being around her. She'd made him feel challenged, engaged, fully alive. He'd always sort of thought she enjoyed it too. Apparently not.

It was a shame, because he could have used some of that good, familiar feeling just now. Sleep hadn't gone well the previous night. His subconscious had decided that what he really needed was one dream after another of that last mission, the one that had cost him everything. It didn't matter that the mission had ended well—he couldn't think of it now without the sick feeling he'd had when his CO told him he couldn't be a SEAL anymore. He'd woken up feeling more tired than he had when he'd gone to bed, like he'd run a hundred miles in his sleep.

"Are you coming?" Kelsey asked from the door of the personnel office. She raised an auburn brow at him, looking impatient.

It took a second for his mind to clear and realize where he was. Not the remote mountains of northern Africa. Not the dead of night, going rogue to save hostages. No. He was home, in Detroit, in an office building, ready to gather information to help solve the final piece of his dad's murder.

Breathe. Just breathe.

He straightened a little, let his hand drop from the wall where he'd braced himself. Good. Good. The inner tension inside him lessened and he could move again. He stepped forward, one foot in front of the other, his old carefree attitude returning with each footfall. He was good at hiding it. Had become a master at it since coming home for his dad's funeral. Didn't have another choice. Because he wanted to keep his shame hidden as long as he could. Not shame, though. No. He wasn't sorry for what he'd done, he just wished it hadn't cost him everything.

Don't get reckless again. Stay focused. Get through this.

By the time he reached Kelsey his mask of confidence was in place, even if he was faking it all.

They walked into the personnel office together and up to a reception desk. Kelsey flashed her credentials while Ryan waited behind her. The woman behind the desk gave them each a flat look. "And he is?"

"A private consultant who's working with me," Kelsey said, as they'd planned.

Meanwhile, Ryan was concentrating on the woman behind the desk. She was the epitome of every disaffected, sour-faced, paper-pushing government employee he'd ever seen in the media. Was that a thing they taught in Marshal school? If so, the woman must have gotten straight As.

Even so, Ryan couldn't resist turning on a bit of his old razzle-dazzle, and before the woman looked away from him again, he couldn't resist winking at her. Getting a rise out of annoying people had always been one of his favorite things in life.

A bit of pink flushed the woman's cheeks and she stared down at her computer screen again.

"We're here to see a file on Kenny Burk, please," Kelsey said. "I think he may be connected to a case I'm working on. I believe he's in undercover work now—or at least, that was the work he began about eight months ago."

The woman behind the desk typed on her computer, then looked up at Kelsey again. "It says here that he put in a request to stop working undercover last month. I'm sorry, but the records don't show where he was transferred to."

"But he's still with the US Marshals?" Ryan asked, stepping forward.

"Again, there's no information that I can share about Marshal Burk's position now," the woman repeated.

"That doesn't make any sense," Ryan said, his tone more forceful now. "You *do* have information about when he was working under-cover, but now that he's not anymore, he's not on the official record? It's got to be in there. Check again."

The woman's mouth puckered even more and one of her eyes twitched. It was very clear that she did not like being questioned—or ordered around. Ryan knew that he should back off, that he should come at this from a different angle, but his bad night of dreams had him totally off his game. And this case meant so much to him that it was hard to deal with someone who was standing in between him and getting answers. He wanted to reach across the reception desk, grab her computer, and shake it until some answers came out—but that would get him thrown out at best and arrested at worst. Ryan tried to take a deep breath so he could calm down and try to fix this mess of a situation, but Kelsey stepped in before he could. Ryan's stomach sank, wondering if she was going to torpedo this situation even further by saying the wrong thing and blowing their cover.

"I apologize for my consultant," she said. "This case is very personal to him, so he gets a little overzealous."

The woman just sniffed in reply. She didn't quite look mollified, but at least she didn't seem to be on the verge of calling in security.

Kelsey balanced her elbow casually on the counter, leaning in closer to the woman. "I have to admit, it's personal for me, too. There's a lot riding on this case, and it's very important to me to get it right. The truth is, I'm going to go out on a limb here and play a hunch about Marshal Burk. If I'm right and he has the information I need about how this case is connected to some of his past work, getting a hold of his location and being able to talk to him could save lives." She leaned closer to the woman, her voice dropping to a conspiratorial whisper. "Just between you and me, I don't have any official backing for tracking down Marshal Burk. My boss doesn't even know I'm here. But it matters to me so much to get this right—to know that I did my job to the absolute best of my ability. That I tried everything I could to keep people safe and to see justice done. I mean, I could be wrong with this hunch. But what if I'm right?" She shrugged and straightened. "I mean, don't you ever just want to trust your instincts? Despite whatever your boss says, because you know you're right?"

The woman behind the desk hesitated, then nodded slowly, giving Kelsey a small smile. "All the time." She glanced back at a closed door behind her, then gestured for Kelsey to lean closer again. "Especially if people's lives are at stake."

Hot damn. Somehow, she'd bonded with this woman. She'd gotten her invested in helping them—and she'd done it without telling a single lie. If anything, the fact that she was so honest and sincere seemed to have helped. Pride swelled up inside Ryan. Kelsey was amazing.

"There really isn't anything in Marshal Burk's file about his transfer location," the woman continued. "Which must mean that it's considered above my pay grade. But I can do a little digging and see what I can find out. Let me look into it for you and I'll be in touch. I want to help you solve your case, Marshal Poppins."

"Thank you." Kelsey slid the woman one of her business cards and they left. Once they were onboard the elevator, Ryan couldn't contain a celebratory whoop.

"Okay. That was amazing. You were amazing back there, Kel. Seriously. Smooth, cool under pressure. And it was so clear how much you care that the woman couldn't help but respond to it. I can see why you're such a good Marshal after all."

"Thanks." She leaned back against the elevator wall and grinned at him. "I wasn't sure it would work, but I just kept thinking that if I could get her to understand why it was so important, she'd want to help. I mean, no one signs up to work for the US Marshals because they *don't* want to make a difference, you know?"

"Well, you rocked it." Ryan gave her a nod. "Once she gets back to us we'll have more to go on. And until then, we can visit the prison where Stephenson died—the prisoner who wasn't transported by Burk or Johnson. If we can prove that Burk was there that day, it'll be another solid tie to prove that he's the one responsible."

"Sounds good," she said, straightening as the elevator dinged their arrival at the lobby once more. "But we'll need to do it tomorrow. I need to get back to the office now."

So, bright and early the next day, Ryan was there to pick up Kelsey in front of the coffee shop near her field office. Apparently, one of the perks of being a Marshal was setting your own schedule. She'd told him that as long as she got her required paperwork done, she could pretty much do as she pleased.

They arrived at FC Milan around ten-thirty and walked up to the visitors desk, asking to see the visitor log for Stephenson on the day that he died. Unfortunately, though, the records weren't available.

"Too far out," the clerk said. "We only keep them on site for ninety days."

"And then?" Ryan asked.

"Well, after that, they go into storage. It's, like, an hour's drive from here, I think? I haven't seen it," the guard admitted. "I-I'm still pretty new. But anyway, once it's all the way out there, the only way you can get a hold of it is with a court order."

Well, fuck.

The kid seemed nervous, fidgety and on edge. One possibility was that he was hiding something—but Ryan didn't actually think that was the case. The guard didn't seem deceptive and he wasn't giving off any of the usual signals that he might be lying. Instead, he just seemed like he was afraid of screwing up. After seeing Kelsey's badge, he was nervous about telling her that he couldn't help her—but on the other hand, he didn't want to hand over any information that he wasn't supposed to hand out. The best way to get through to him, Ryan sensed, was to take the soft approach, ease his nerves. Thankfully, he'd slept much better the previous night, so he was able to take point on this one—though he decided to follow Kelsey's lead, use the sincerity that had worked so well the previous day.

"I get that this stuff is all confidential. Need to know basis and all that." He smiled. "You want to follow the rules," he said. "Do everything right. I get it. Hey, I've been there myself. We don't want you to cross any lines. But this information could make such a big difference for us, you know? We really would appreciate any help you could give. This job means a lot to you, doesn't it? Well, our job means a lot to us, too—and we really want to get this right."

The young guard swallowed hard, his Adam's apple bobbing in his skinny neck. He looked maybe a few years younger than Ryan, age-wise, and a world away experience-wise. Finally, he ducked his head a little and looked away. Bingo. Ryan had hit his target. "I replaced another guard who died in a drunk driving accident. He screwed up. I don't want to make that kind of mistake. I need this job. But..." He glanced around, then started typing on his keyboard, his fingers fumbling slightly from nerves, Ryan supposed. "To help out fellow law enforcement, let me check one other place."

Hope quickly fizzled, however, when he came back, shaking his head. "Sorry. I checked the backups, but they've been purged."

"What about surveillance footage?" Kelsey asked, moving closer to Ryan. "Would there be any of that kept we could look at?"

The guy gave her a quick glance, then started typing again. "No.

Looks like that's been purged too. We have so much of it that we can't keep it all forever."

"Understood." She leaned back and sighed, turning her attention to Ryan. "What next?"

"We keep looking." He thanked the guard, then walked out the front entrance with Kelsey.

"I don't know where else to dig," she said as they walked to his car. "Everything we've tried so far had been a dead end. Well, except for ruling out Phil as a suspect." She sighed as she climbed into the passenger seat and buckled her seatbelt while he did the same behind the wheel and started the engine. "Maybe I should loop in one of my coworkers on this. Get some fresh eyes on the case."

"No," Ryan said emphatically as they pulled out of the fenced-in lot. "We can't loop anybody else in at this point because we don't know who else might be involved. For now, it's safer if we keep our circle tight."

She shook her head and stared out the window beside her, expression discouraged. "But if we don't open up some, we'll never get this case solved."

Ryan didn't say anything—but he didn't have to. They both knew she was right.

5

———————

S aturday morning, they met at the coffee shop again. The place was packed, but Ryan had gotten there early, thank goodness, and gotten them a booth near the windows in the back for some privacy. Kelsey gave him a small wave when she walked in, ignoring the inconvenient way her heart stumbled whenever she saw him. She was not attracted to him. She wasn't. And even if she was, she refused to let it go anywhere. A relationship with him would spell disaster with a capital D. They didn't like each other, not really. They were polar opposites in their personalities. It could never go anywhere.

Could it?

No, it couldn't. No matter how good he looked, or how amazing it made her feel when he praised her at the personnel office the other day, or how surprisingly fun it was to work with him and bounce ideas off of him. They were incompatible, and that was that. She shook off the thought and ordered her double soy latte with hazelnut flavoring and a healthy bran muffin, then moved down the counter to pay and wait, forcing herself to think about all the reasons why she should *not* pursue her attraction to Ryan. What she needed was to go have dinner

38

at her parents' house this week and get a good old-fashioned dose of common sense from them. Usually she tried to go once a week, since they lived in town, but she'd been so busy lately, she'd missed the past week. Okay. Fine. The past few weeks, but they were fine with it. In fact, her mom had texted her earlier telling her to have a good day and that she loved her. With a smiley face even.

"Kelsey," the guy behind the counter called and Kelsey stepped up to grab her stuff, then weaved through the crowded tables over to Ryan. From the snippets of conversation she heard around her, it was a lot of college kids in there today, and a few groups of women getting ready to go on shopping sprees at the outlet mall a few towns over. She slid into her side of the booth, careful not to brush legs with him under the table, then made the mistake of looking at him. God, it should be illegal for a man to look that good so early in the morning. Dressed as usual in a T-shirt and jeans, this time with a sweater pulled haphazardly over the top, he could have walked right out of one of those magazine ads with the casually gorgeous guy just sprawling over who knew where. Kelsey gulped her hot coffee, glad for the distracting scald on her throat. Eyes watering, she blinked fast and asked him, "How's it going?"

"Good." Ryan dunked his pastry into his coffee and took a bite, then wiped his mouth and swallowed before saying, "I've been thinking about the whole fresh eyes thing and letting people in, and I think I might have a compromise that would work."

"Yeah?" Kelsey couldn't help noticing a pastry crumb near the corner of Ryan's mouth and feeling an insane urge to reach over and brush it off for him. Or even worse, lick it off with her tongue. She clenched her free hand beneath the table and drank more coffee. Dammit. She needed to stop thoughts like that, especially after that crazy kiss they'd shared. They were working together on this case, and that was all. No sexy times allowed. Nope. Not even in her head. Not even when that kiss had been the best one she'd had in years, maybe ever.

Ryan Ward was not the man for her. Now, if she could just get that through to her errant libido, she'd be all set. Kelsey took a bite of her bran muffin, chewing an inordinate amount of time before swallowing, not trusting her words. Then she cleared her suddenly constricted throat and frowned down at the worn tabletop. Focus on the work. The work always saved her. "Really? What kind of compromise is it?"

"Well, my brother Neal and his fiancée, Lori, run my dad's old PI office, Ward Investigation. Lori's a licensed PI. Neal isn't yet, but he's working on it. I called him already and asked him if he'd be willing to take a look at the case for us, and he said he would. We're scheduled to meet him at their offices in about an hour."

"Oh, uh…" At first, her brain sort of short-circuited for a second. Her first instinct was to be annoyed that he hadn't asked her first before arranging the meeting, but then she realized that this could be the break they needed, so she let it go. "Wow. Okay. And Neal was okay with it all? I mean, I've only met him that one time, at the range and then while we were having drinks, but he didn't seem all that enthusiastic about the idea of you chasing down this lead with the Marshals' office. I kind of got the sense that it was your baby."

Ryan shrugged. "It is. Lori and Neal already did their part for the case. If it wasn't for Lori, we wouldn't have even realized what really happened to Dad. The coroner thought it was a heart attack—Lori was the only one who suspected that it might be murder. She and Neal went through hell finding the truth. But that was enough for them— finding the guy responsible. They've moved on to other clients, other cases. I'm the one who wants to see this through and solve the last piece of the puzzle."

He looked so sad, thinking about his father, that she started to reach out to take his hand. She caught herself and held back, remembering her resolve to keep her distance, but then… *Fuck it.* It wasn't a question of falling for him—it was just showing some basic human compassion. He deserved that just as much as anyone. She reached over and placed her hand on his, squeezing gently. His eyes flew up to meet hers, genuine shock written all over his face in a way that made her heart clench harder. Was he really that unaccustomed to anyone reaching out to him?

He turned his hand over under hers to squeeze her hand back, then pulled away, picking up his coffee cup like he wanted to hide behind it. Finally, he cleared his throat and spoke again.

"Anyway, his main objection to getting involved was that he didn't think we had enough evidence, but then I showed him those printouts of the transport records, and that was enough to get him to revise his opinion and agree to help." Ryan gave her a confident grin and her pulse kicked up a notch despite her wishes. "I'll convince him more when we get there. I'm good at that."

Yeah. He was. Too good.

Once they were finished, they threw away their trash, then headed out to her car. Apparently the Ward Investigation offices were a little tricky to get to, so he'd insisted on riding with her so that he could give her directions. They climbed in and she started the car.

Ryan glanced into the backseat and laughed. "Have a party in here last night or something?"

"Huh." She scrunched her nose and looked where he was pointing. An empty vodka bottle lay on the back seat. Turning back to Ryan, Kelsey shook her head in genuine confusion. "That's not mine."

"Uh huh. Sure." Ryan continued giving her a hard time as they pulled out of the lot and headed toward his brother's office. "I'm seeing all sorts of new sides to you, Marshal Poppins."

"I'm telling you, it's not mine. I have no idea how it could have gotten in there. Maybe I left the window rolled down and someone threw it in? Weird prank, though." She signaled and merged into the left lane.

"Pull over."

Kelsey scowled over at him. "What? I can't just pull over here. There's traffic and rules and—"

"I don't give a shit," he said, glancing in his side mirror. "Next lane's clear. Pull over now, right there, before we get to the intersection."

She glanced up ahead, where a brick wall sat on the other side of the roadway, forcing you to go either right or left. She wasn't sure exactly what Ryan's problem was, but she'd already realized that his instincts were usually correct. She signaled again and eased over into the right lane, tapping the brakes. Except nothing happened. Fuck.

Kelsey tried the brakes again. Still nothing. The car was drifting right now, and though they weren't going that fast—maybe 35 mph—there was a tree dead ahead in front of them next to the curb. It was only remembering her defensive driving training that made her swerve in time to miss it. Thankfully, there weren't any pedestrians on the side-walk, because they ended up going up over the curb and finally coming to a gentle stop with the front bumper resting against the corner of a storefront. No damage done, other than to her composure.

Hands shaking, Kelsey cut the engine, then just sat there, eyes wide with disbelief. "What the actual hell is going on?"

Ryan released his white-knuckled grip on the dashboard and sat back, breathing faster than normal. The incident itself wasn't that scary, per se, but the implications were, as evidenced by his next words. "I think someone's trying to kill you, Kel."

Her mind had zoomed there too, of course, but then ricocheted off. That couldn't be it. Who would want her dead? She was just a low-level Marshal. She wasn't working on any high-profile, high-stakes cases—except that she *was,* wasn't she? Even if it wasn't official, she was looking into a multiple homicide. If whoever had killed all of those prison inmates realized she was looking into him, then who knew what he'd do? He'd already proven he was willing to kill. The realization was both chilling and horrifying.

"You knew this would happen?" she asked. "Just from a vodka bottle?"

"I hoped I was wrong," Ryan admitted. "And since you were able to drive to the coffee shop this morning without any problems, I thought maybe it was a problem that wasn't supposed to show up right away. My plan was for you to pull over so I could check for some of the more obvious issues and get things fixed *before* the brakes failed, or the motherboard fried, or the engine gave out. I didn't realize the situation was already that bad. But yeah, I had my suspicions that something was wrong. No one would just throw a vodka bottle into your car for no reason. But if someone planted it there, hoping to make any accident you were in look like a case of drunk driving…"

Her stomach lurched and she swallowed hard to keep her breakfast down. Oh God.

"I need to call Neal and tell him what's happened," Ryan said, pulling out his phone and glancing over at her. "It's okay, Kelsey. It's going to be okay."

But how could it be okay? Someone had tried to murder her just now. She shuddered despite herself and Ryan reached over to take her hand, hitting speed dial for his brother with the other. He put the call on speakerphone so they could both hear it.

"Ward Investigation," his brother answered on the second ring.

"Hey, Neal, it's Ryan. We've got a situation here."

His brother's tone turned from friendly to focused in seconds. "What kind of a situation? Are you hurt?"

Ryan looked over at Kelsey again, then shook his head. "No. We're fine, but there's been an accident. I'm pretty sure the brake lines were cut in Kelsey's car."

"Shit," Neal said.

"Yep. Shit is right. Because that means that someone else has found out about us investigating and they're not happy about it."

Kelsey tensed slightly hearing him say it out loud, even though deep down she knew it was true.

"Have you called the police yet?" Neal asked over the phone line. "If not, let me call it in for you. I've got a contact in the department who has handled the other cases tying back to Dad. He'll want to know about this." He took a deep breath. "So, yeah, Ryan. I'd say your hunch about the Marshals is probably correct. You guys sit tight and wait for the police to get there. I'm making the call now."

Ryan hung up, then leaned his head back against the headrest to stare up at the ceiling, still holding her hand, like he needed the contact as much as she did. "Well, this morning didn't go like I'd planned."

Despite the circumstances, Kelsey snorted. It all still felt a little unbe-lievable, but one thing stayed rock-solid in her head. "Pretty sure an attempt on my life means it's time to go to Internal Affairs with this, evidence or not."

He chuckled, then nodded. "Yep. I think you're right."

6

———————

Bright and early Monday morning, Ryan was on his way over to pick Kelsey up so they could go to Internal Affairs. He was feeling pretty good about things, at least until he received a phone call, as he was pulling into her driveway, from his old CO.

Throat tight, Ryan pulled into a parking spot, then answered. "Hello?"

"Ward, this is Elderman. I've got the date for your formal discharge hearing."

Shit. Ryan had been trying to keep busy so he wouldn't have to think about it. But yeah. While he'd been told that his time in the navy was over, there was still a lot of paperwork and red tape in order for him to be formally discharged from his SEAL team. He put the call on speaker, then scrambled to open his calendar on his phone while Elderman rattled off a date for the following month. All the while, he was painfully aware of Kelsey standing just outside her apartment building, watching him, clearly sensing that he wasn't ready for her to join him.

Fuck it all to hell and back.

Cursing under his breath, he entered the info his CO gave him. Even though he'd been expecting it, the call came as a real kick in the gut. Just one more reminder of everything he'd lost.

"You'll get an official notice in the mail in a few days," Elderman said. "I'm sorry it had to go this way, son."

Ryan tried to swallow down the lump in his throat. "Yeah. Me, too, sir." The call ended quickly after that.

He took a deep breath, then another, trying to get his head back in the game and focus on the case. Once his pulse slowed and his stomach stopped aching, he gestured for Kelsey to come get in the car. They had work to do.

By the time they were at the Internal Affairs office, Ryan had almost put the call and the hearing out of his mind completely. Almost. It still lurked around the edges, in the shadows, but not enough that he couldn't keep functioning at top performance where his dad's case was concerned.

He and Kelsey told the Marshal investigating the accident about everything they knew so far—his reasons for believing a Marshal was behind the "heart attack" deaths of the prisoners, the evidence she had found in the transport files that showed who had had contact with those prisoners on the days that they died, and finally what had happened on Saturday, with the planted vodka bottle in the backseat and the mechanic's report that someone had deliberately frayed the brake lines.

"I see," the Marshal behind the desk said. Weldon, according to the name plaque on the desk. "Well, Mr. Ward, Marshal Poppins, we'll take all this under review."

"Review?" Ryan glanced at Kelsey, who was sitting next to him in front of the desk. "What does that mean?"

"It means that you need to leave this all with us and we'll take over the investigation from here." The woman reached into her desk and passed a card to Kelsey. "Marshal Poppins, my email is there at the bottom. If you could forward all the files you have on this to me, I'd appreciate it."

Well, fuck.

There went his plans to keep busy with the investigation until his hearing. And sure, he understood procedure and all, but it didn't help him much. Without the case, what the hell was he going to do with himself?

Sit around twiddling his thumbs until his hearing, that's what.

His rapidly souring mood turned even worse.

They walked out of the IA offices, located on a different floor of the Federal Building downtown, then back to their car.

"Hey," Kelsey said once they'd climbed back inside his vehicle and he'd started the engine. "Want to tell me what's wrong with you today?"

"Nothing wrong with me," he grumbled, checking his mirrors and signaling before pulling out into traffic. "Why?"

"I don't know," she said, staring straight ahead. "Maybe because you look like a walking, talking thundercloud? I'm almost afraid to ask you anything for fear you'll rip my head off."

"I'm just in a bad mood, is all," he conceded, doing his best not to scowl and failing.

"Okay. Why?"

"Why are you asking me all the questions?" He gave her a look as they slowed for a red light.

"Because we're partners in this case and I don't want you flipping out and going rogue on me because you're pissed off about something I don't know about."

Ouch. Nice to know where they stood—and that she thought he was capable of going on some kind of violent spree just because he was in a shitty mood. Jaw tight, he gripped the steering wheel hard and accelerated once the light turned green, heading back through town toward her field office to drop her off for work. He felt like the weight of the world was on his shoulders and it would crush him if he didn't get it off him. But there was no one he could talk to, no way to ask anyone to share the load. No way in hell could he talk to his brothers about this shit, no matter how many times they asked. It wasn't that he didn't trust them—but he knew they just wouldn't understand. Perfect SEALs, both of them, following the rules, doing the right thing. Never screwing up. Not like him.

"Ryan?" Kelsey said again, gentler this time. "It's not just that. I care about you. Seriously. As a friend. If you need someone to talk to, I'm here."

With a sigh, he laid out the bare details for her. "I got my date this morning for when I have to return to base. For my formal discharge hearing. I was hoping that the investigation would keep me busy so I wouldn't have to think about it, but IA just took the case out of our hands, which means I've got nothing to do until then but sit around and stew over it."

"Oh." She took that in a moment before asking, "Is that normal? The discharge hearing."

"Yeah, it's…it's procedure. Got to dot all the 'i's and cross the 't's. It's not enough to just say that I can't be in the navy anymore because I fucked up." She let out a soft sound of protest but didn't say anything.

They drove on in silence for a few minutes, as her words looped in his head.

If you need someone to talk to, I'm here…

And man. He really did need someone to talk to. More than he'd realized.

Maybe that was why he decided to finally open up to her about what was going on. Well, that and for some odd reason, he felt like he could trust her with his secrets. She was a good listener and he'd been carrying this so long. He was tired. Exhausted.

Finally, he pulled over in a grocery store parking lot and spilled the whole story.

"I'd just found out that Dad died, but I was on a mission in Northern Africa and had to stuff my feelings about that to do my job and carry out my duty," he said, the memories of that time resurfacing to play like a movie in his mind. "We were there to rescue some hostages, a group of international medical aid workers. Some warlord had captured them, was holding them hostage. We were all ready to go in and get them, but then the mission got scrubbed at the last minute."

Kelsey was watching him intently, giving him her full attention. "Why?" she asked.

He shrugged. "The higher-ups said there was too much cloud cover and it would be better to wait for a night later on in the week when we could have the benefit of drones to scout ahead for us." He took a deep breath, his inner tension building. "But the thing is, in the most recent ransom video I'd seen something that made me think that the warlord was going to kill those hostages soon, before we could get back in there to get them."

"What did you see?" Kelsey asked, turning slightly to see him better. "A sign? A secret signal?"

"Sort of." He smiled, for real this time. She looked so cute when she was all interested in something. He took another deep breath to focus his thoughts back on his story and away from the woman beside him. "One of the hostages, this woman named Mary—she had a habit of nodding along in the hostage videos the warlord made them film. A different hostage—Frank—would read the list of demands and say they were going to be released as soon as the warlord's demands were met. And Mary would just nod along. I don't think it was even conscious on her part, but I'd noticed it, all the same. And then, in the more recent video we'd watched, Mary wasn't nodding. Instead, she gave a tiny, barely-there-if-you-weren't-looking-for-it headshake when Frank read the part about them all being released alive."

"Wow. That sounds important."

"I thought so. It seemed like one of those things my dad used to tell me about—how people tell you everything you need to know, if you just pay attention and catch on to what to watch for. It felt so obvious to me…but no one else agreed." He huffed out a breath. At her wince, he nodded. "Yep. Anyway, I was certain of what I'd seen and my gut told me I was right. So, I decided to disobey orders and lead the rescue mission as planned. I saved the hostages, no one on my SEAL team was hurt, and the mission got positive international attention— lots of good press for the navy."

"You know, now that you mention it, I do remember hearing some-thing about that on the news," Kelsey said, sitting back. "I didn't know you were involved, though. I assume you going off on your own to do that didn't sit well with your higher-ups?"

"Uh, no. That's putting it mildly." Ryan chuckled. "I think there were at least a few who wanted to hang me out to dry for disobeying orders. But my CO had my back, saying that I'd been compromised due to 'mental distress.' He argued for having me get a mental health discharge instead of having me flat-out court-martialed—and eventually, he got everyone else to agree. That was when it was over for me, really, even if the paperwork still had to process through. He told me to come home for the funeral and stay here, that he'd let me know when to report for my discharge hearing. Which he just did." He reached into his jeans pocket with one hand and pulled out a medallion to hand to Kelsey. "One of the hostages gave me that, after the rescue, to thank me. It's a St. Jude medallion. The patron saint of lost causes." He laughed. "Fitting, right? I've kept it with me ever since."

Kelsey studied the medallion, then handed it back to him.

"Look," he continued, putting the medallion back in his pocket. "I know I got off easy. The mission could have easily gone wrong. People could have died, and it would have all been on me. Or I could have ended up court-martialed after all. This—successful mission, no casualties, honorable discharge—is about as well as things could have gone. But it still feels like getting the rug pulled out from under me every time I think about it. And especially today, when I got that call from my CO. I mean, I feel ashamed to have been kicked out of my SEAL team and the Navy, especially when both of my brothers severed honorably. Neal got medically discharged after an injury and Lance is retiring from his desk job at the Pentagon." Ryan sighed again, then made a right turn onto the street where the field offices were located. "I guess I thought as long as I always gave the mission in front of me everything I had, and focused on it exclusively, I'd succeed. But that's what I did on that mission and I still lost my military career, my teammates, and my sense of purpose, all in one go."

Now that it was all out there, he felt oddly empty. Ryan waited for Kelsey to tell him he was a fool or an idiot for disobeying orders. Instead, she surprised him. Again.

"Were you right?" she asked, staring down at her hands in her lap.

"What?"

"Were you right?" she repeated, looking up at him again. No judgment in those lovely brown eyes, just keen curiosity. "That they were going to execute the hostages?"

It took him a moment, but Ryan nodded. "Yeah, I was. They interviewed the hostages afterward, along with the captured warlord, and everyone agreed that that had been the plan."

"Well, then." She took a deep breath. "I'd say you're a hero for saving a lot of lives."

Ryan snorted, then hung his head. "Yeah, in a perfect world, maybe, I could've shared my hunch and the higher-ups would've reinstated the mission and I wouldn't have had to choose between insubordination and saving lives." He shrugged and stared out the windshield. "But sometimes missions aren't so black and white, and they're certainly never perfect. Nothing is. Life is messy."

"Maybe." She reached over and put her hand atop his, her skin warm and soft against him. "But in my book, at least, it sounds like you did the best you could in a complicated situation and your actions deserve commendation, not discharge." Kelsey stared at him a second, the weight of it burning a hole in the side of his head because he couldn't look at her right then. If he did, he might lose it, or else pull her into his lap and kiss her silly for believing in him. Neither action was acceptable to him, so he stayed where he was, keeping it all inside as always. Finally, she sighed and checked her watch. "Shit. I need to get to work."

He started the car back up and drove her the rest of the way to her office. When they arrived, she reached over and gave his hand another squeeze. "I'll call you later, okay?"

He gave a curt nod, then watched as she got out of the car and walked inside her office building. Ryan sat there in the parking lot for a while afterward. Shockingly, he felt better after having told Kelsey about what was going on with him. But he also felt raw and vulnerable inside. Way more vulnerable than he had in a long time. And while he didn't regret talking to Kelsey about stuff, his instinct was to withdraw now for a bit, get back to his comfort zone of focusing on the investigation so he could function again.

7

Ryan spent a chunk of the day puttering around his dad's house, trying to figure out what to do with himself. He wanted to work on the case, but he couldn't think of any leads to follow. He knew he probably *ought* to begin thinking about what the hell he was going to do with himself after his discharge hearing. But honestly, he just didn't know. Or more accurately, he didn't want to think about it. But now that he had a definite date, it was something he needed to think about. That, and the fact he'd have to come clean with his brothers about it all too. His stomach cramped at the thought. He hated disappointing people, especially his family. And while he still didn't regret his actions on that ill-fated mission, he wished it had all turned out differently for him. His brothers were the closest people in the world to him now, with his dad gone, and he didn't want to do anything to screw up those relationships, especially now that they were back together again.

The phone ringing was a welcome distraction, especially when he saw that the call was coming from Kelsey.

"Hey," she said, the sounds of traffic echoing behind her down the phone line telling him she was outside the office. "I just got an anonymous email at work from someone who says they heard we're looking for Kenny Burk. They said they're an undercover Marshal who worked with Kenny undercover and they have information about what he's doing now. They're willing to meet with me, but only this afternoon, for an hour, at an address across town. I looked it up and it's an apartment building."

"Shit," he said, for lack of anything better, his mind still lost in the past. He shook off those thoughts as best he could and concentrated on what Kelsey was saying. "Give me the address."

She did and he googled it on his phone right then. Huh. From what he could tell, the place had been condemned a while ago, which meant if someone wanted to meet her there, chances were high it was shady as fuck. His SEAL instincts went on high alert, the same way they did on missions where probability was high they were walking into a trap.

"Yeah," Kelsey said, breaking him out of his thoughts. "I know it sounds weird, but it also sounds like a lead, so I'm not sure we can afford to ignore it. I mean, I know we're supposed to be off the case, but they said they'd only meet with me, so…"

"No. You're right. We do need intel. But I'm coming with you." The SEAL-trained gears in his head began to turn as he thought through possible motives, outcomes, and responses. Strategy was kind of his thing on his SEAL team. He was good at visualizing outcomes and figuring out what they needed to do to get there. "Okay, we meet this lead in person. See if they're legit and if their intel is useful. If it is, then we can pass that on to Internal Affairs." He stood and walked over to shove on his shoes. "Sit tight. I'll be there in fifteen minutes."

Once he'd strapped on his holstered weapon and made sure his phone was fully charged, Ryan headed over to pick up Kelsey and they drove to the address the person had given them. Along the way, they made idle small talk, chatting about the weather or the case or pretty much anything but the sizzling awareness between them. He'd done his best to ignore it, knowing it was not a good idea to get involved with Kelsey beyond this case, but damn if it wasn't getting harder and harder to think about anything else. Up until now, he'd been certain that his lifestyle was incompatible with any kind of relationship. He was all about the work, all about completing the missions. Growing up, he'd watched his dad run a successful detective agency, but fail completely in his personal life. Even Lance, his older brother, had had issues with balancing a personal and a professional life. He'd done great in ROTC in high school and had a stellar military career in the SEALs, but his marriage to his high school sweetheart, Ruth, had crashed and burned. Of the three of them, Neal had probably made the wisest choice. He'd waited until he was out of the military, medically discharged from his SEAL team due to an injury, before ever really dating or getting involved with someone seriously. Ryan figured he'd follow the same path someday, once he was done in the SEALs.

But then, well, his military career had flamed out. Technically, he was free to do whatever he wanted with his life now, but that didn't do any good when he didn't know what the hell he wanted. Until he got himself straightened out, chasing after a romance seemed like a terrible idea.

He pulled into the pockmarked parking lot and stopped in a slot near a bunch of heavy construction equipment, his chest tight and his heart heavy. But now wasn't the time to deal with his emotional shit. Now was the time to work. An easy escape? Maybe. But a necessary one, for now.

Ryan peered out the windshield at the apartment building before them. From the outside, it looked just like any other slightly dilapidated gray stone building in the city. Many of these places were being torn down to make room for new construction. Based on the signage and equipment parked around this one, it would be no different. From what he could tell, demolition hadn't started yet, but the fact that it clearly would soon told him all he needed to know about the bad shape the building was in. It wasn't like he'd expected their mysterious source to meet them at the Ritz-Carlton with a billboard proclaiming their identity, but anyone who watched any sort of horror movie knew that bad things happened in abandoned buildings.

He pulled out his sidearm and checked it, making sure the magazine was fully loaded before slamming it back into the butt of his Glock. Kelsey did the same with her gun. Then they exchanged a look and a nod before exiting the vehicle, both in full mission mode now. Some people might have thought it weird, how they were able to instantly shut off everything else like that to focus on the situation at hand, but it was part of the job. For a SEAL or a US Marshal, he supposed. It was a thing you learned early on and did routinely, to stay sane and stay alert.

Moving cautiously and scanning their surroundings as they went, he and Kelsey ducked under the caution tape, then found an opening in the chain link fence marking the perimeter of the site. They slipped through, then headed to the glass double doors at the front entrance of the building. Ryan gave Kelsey another look, then tried the handle, expecting it to be locked, but it wasn't. Another red flag.

His not-okay meter notched higher. Something was definitely up here. The smart move would probably be to retreat—but this was the best lead they currently had and Ryan just couldn't bring himself to walk away. He tried to convince himself that as long as he stayed alert, he'd be able to deal with whatever trouble was almost certainly coming for them.

"Where exactly did they say they'd meet us?" Ryan asked as they slowly went inside. The air was thick with dust and who knew what else. His eyes began to itch almost immediately and it felt like his skin was coated with ick. He had no idea exactly when this place had been built, but from the looks of it, it had been shut down a long, long time —and probably should have been *torn* down a while ago. He almost pulled his T-shirt up to cover his nose and mouth, but figured they wouldn't be there long. He'd survived worse, though he tried to take slow, shallow breaths to avoid getting too much gunk in his lungs.

"Let me check the email again. It said the first floor, I remember." Kelsey said, pulling out her phone. "No. Sorry. The basement. It says a studio apartment in the basement—*the* studio apartment, so I guess there's only one." She squinted through the shadowed lobby, then pointed. "Over there. There's a sign with an arrow that says basement."

They started that way, guns still at low ready, just in case, picking their way past old rolls of carpet and hunks of concrete and fallen ceiling tiles. The steps, thankfully, were sturdy enough, and it didn't take them long to find the studio apartment in question. The door was already open, just waiting for them. They peered inside cautiously, not sure what they'd find.

The good news was that it was bare—no broken furniture or other debris, nothing that could cover a trap or serve as a hiding place for an attacker. The bad news was that it was bare—no sign of the person they were supposed to be meeting.

"Wait, there's a paper over there in the corner," Kelsey pointed out. "Do you think it could be a note?"

"I'll check it out," Ryan volunteered, stepping slowly into the room, on high alert. Kelsey waited for him in the doorway. Ryan's full attention was on the paper, but he spun around in a hurry when he heard Kelsey shriek, followed by a thud—and then a slam. When he looked over, he saw Kelsey on the floor, groaning a little as she sat up. The door to the apartment was now closed.

"What happened?" he demanded.

"Someone shoved me," she said as she got to her feet. "I didn't see who." She went over to the door and tried to open it, but whoever closed it must have locked or jammed it. Ryan hurried over to try for himself, but he didn't have any luck either.

"Well, shit," he said. "So we're trapped in here?"

"Looks that way," she agreed, then frowned. "Uh, do you smell that?" She sniffed, then gasped. "Smells like rotten eggs. It's natural gas. It's probably been leaking since before we came in, but it wasn't as noticeable with the door open."

Ryan took a sniff and coughed, his pulse pounding. "You're right. We need to get out of here. Now!" Whoever had locked them in here wasn't just trying to trap them. They were trying to kill them. He turned back to the door again. Since the knob wouldn't turn, the best option would be to take it off the hinges, but he didn't have the tools. He looked around for any other exit, and saw that the one window was high up on the wall, near the ceiling. It was also boarded up. The door still seemed like the best bet. He managed to locate a piece of plywood and a hammer the demolition crew must have left behind, and began to bang on the pins to get them out. "See if you can find the leak," he told Kelsey. "Maybe we can shut it off before it gets too bad, or seal it up with something to buy us some time. Whatever you do, be careful. One spark and this place goes up like a bomb."

In fact, he probably shouldn't be banging metal on metal with the hammer either, so he put that aside and just used the wood. Not nearly as effective, but with the advantage of them not going boom.

As he worked, to no avail, the rotten egg smell just got stronger, to the point that Ryan was feeling lightheaded and nauseous. The studio apartment was small—it wouldn't take long at all for the gas to fill it past the point of no return. Kelsey was hacking and gagging, too, and the hinge pins hadn't budged at all.

"We have to try the window," Kelsey called out. "If you get me up on your shoulders, I should be able to reach."

Getting her up in position wasn't easy—Ryan's head was swimming and he was seriously worried about dropping her—but they got her in place, with the hammer in her hand to pry the boards loose. He heard her hissing in pain and knew that the rough boards were probably tearing her hands, but there was nothing he could do except hold as still and as stable as possible. Kelsey gave a cry of triumph as the boards finally came loose. She was able to smash the window open with the hammer, which made Ryan breathe a little easier, literally and figuratively. From there, it was easy enough to boost her through the opening and outside. After that, she was able to give him a hand up and help him pull himself through, as well.

They both lay on the dusty pavement outside, gasping and gagging, and staring up at the gray, cloudy sky above, breathing in deep lungfuls of clean, crisp air. They were both scraped up from the broken glass, queasy from the gas, and light-headed from the adrenaline, but they were *alive.* In spite of everything, they were alive.

"Man, that was a close call," Kelsey said, after a long moment, her voice scratchy.

"No shit." Ryan took a deep breath before sitting up. He still felt a bit shaky, but way better than before. The rotten egg smell lingered still out here, though not nearly as badly. They'd have to call in the fire department to get that shut off safely. He hung his head and scrubbed a hand through his hair. "Really makes you take stock of things, facing danger and possible death like that, huh?"

"Yeah." Kelsey had her eyes closed, her face so sweet and serene that he almost leaned in and kissed her before he stopped himself. *Stop looking at her mouth. Stop it.* "It really does."

Distracted, he looked away fast and stared at an ant on the pavement, hauling off a leaf ten times its size. He knew how that felt, carrying a huge burden like that. Ryan sighed. "Made me think of all the stuff I haven't done yet," he said. He tucked his knees in tighter to his chest and gripped them with his hands to keep from reaching for her. Whatever it was, he couldn't seem to stop himself from talking. "Like all the stuff I've been putting off doing until after I got out of the military. Get married. Start a family. Create a good life for myself as a civilian."

Kelsey leaned into him, smiling and nudging him with her shoulder. "Listen to you, going all soft on me. But I know what you mean. I feel like I should go skydiving or visit the Grand Canyon or swim with dolphins or something right now, you know? Cross something off my bucket list. Do something I almost never got the chance to do."

Yes, that was it exactly. He'd felt like his life was over when he'd lost his position with his SEAL team, but this brush with death had shown him that it wasn't. He was still alive. And he wanted to do something that made him *feel* alive.

Without another thought in his mind, he turned and kissed her. And damn, it was good. Better than good. It was amazing. Even better than their first kiss in her office. He turned slightly to get a better angle. then deepened it, taking advantage of her surprised gasp to sweep his tongue into her mouth. She moaned low in her throat, the sound zinging straight to his groin, then wrapped her free arm around his neck, pulling him close, like she couldn't get enough of him either.

Then, as fast as it had started, Ryan pulled back. As much as he wanted to continue, this place wasn't safe for them. Not at all. He rested his forehead against Kelsey's a second, their breaths mingling, before he pulled away and clambered to his feet, holding out a hand to help her up. "We need to get out of here. Whoever locked that door could still be around and neither of us is in shape to fight anyone right now."

8

———————

Once they were back at her apartment, Kelsey called the police to report the gas leak. After she'd ended the call, she leaned against the wall to steady herself. Between the fumes she'd inhaled and the kiss with Ryan, she felt completely discombobulated. Normally, she'd take a quiet bath and center herself, but Ryan was still here and wanted to talk about the case. So she took a deep, cleansing breath, then walked back into the living room where he was sitting on one end of her sofa, looking at the copies of the case files she'd kept for herself.

"So this was clearly another attempt to stop us from investigating—but what does it tell us?" He scowled down at the paperwork. "How can we use this to solve my dad's case once and for all?"

Kelsey plopped down on the opposite end of the sofa from him and picked up one of the papers from the table. "Well, for starters, whoever did this knows that we're looking for Kenny. Otherwise, they wouldn't have known to use that as bait for the trap. But I'm not sure if that's really much of a clue. We've told a number of people that we're looking for him. And who knows who those people might have mentioned it to?"

Ryan made a face. "Fair point. Okay, so that doesn't necessarily lead us to any answers. How about theories? Could it have been Kenny himself who locked us in?"

"Could be," she agreed. "I didn't see who pushed me, but whoever it was seemed strong, solid. That would fit Kenny." Her eyes widened as a new idea occurred. "Or maybe there really was a source who wanted to talk to us, but Kenny or someone working with him found out about the meeting, scared them off, then locked us inside." She straightened. "We should go back there, after the cops clear it, and check if any of the nearby buildings have surveillance cameras."

"Hmm. Good idea." Ryan sat back and shifted slightly to face her. "I think we need to find out if anyone in the Marshals service ever lived in that building. That basement apartment was a good trap. Whoever sent us there was familiar enough with the space to know how to rig the gas. It would make sense if they were a former tenant. It's a long shot, but something." He set his own paper aside. "And I think you should follow up with our contact in the personnel office to see if she's made any headway with figuring out where Kenny disappeared to."

"On it," she said, pulling out her phone again and dialing the number. It wasn't quite five o'clock yet, so maybe she could still catch the woman. But no. Straight to voicemail. She left a message, checking in, then ended the call. "Done."

"Great. Next I think—" Ryan started.

"Next I think we need to talk about what happened, outside, after we escaped," Kelsey said. She'd never been one to dance around a subject and she wasn't about to start now. Clear and direct was always the best policy in her book. "Why did you kiss me back there? Was it just an affirmation of life thing or something more?"

Ryan looked speechless, for the first time since she'd known him, and that was saying something. He blinked at her, hesitating, then exhaled slowly and leaned his shoulder into the cushions. "I don't know, Kelsey. I guess it was something more. I mean, the close call did have me thinking about all the things I wanted that I've been putting off, but it wasn't just about wanting a kiss. It meant more than that."

She scooted closer, sensing she was on to something big here, the anticipation inside her swelling to uncomfortable proportions. It was like the very air between them was charged with possibilities, and her heart was racing and her breath caught in her chest, hanging on his next words. "What is it that you want, Ryan?"

He caught her gaze, held. Time seemed to slow and her lips tingled with expectation of another searing kiss from him…but no. Ryan turned back to the coffee table, his frown deepening as he pulled away from her, both physically and emotionally. "It doesn't matter what I want, Kelsey. We need to focus on my dad's case."

"The case can wait," she said, with more force than she'd intended, but dammit. It felt like she was dangling by a string here and he was the puppet master, and she didn't like it one bit. "Tell me what you want, Ryan."

Cursing under his breath, he slammed the papers down on the table with more force than necessary and whispered, "You. I want you, Kelsey. Okay? Satisfied?"

"Nope. Not by a long shot." And then she was on him, like white on rice, practically climbing him as she tackled him back into the sofa cushions with her kiss, scrambling up onto his lap to straddle him. She felt almost frantic, but damn, she wanted him too. She hadn't even realized how much until this moment. It was like a switch had been flipped and her libido was firing on all cylinders now. She was desperate for him, craved him more than her next breath. And Kelsey was going to have him too. Right here, right now.

Between kisses, Ryan somehow managed to get them lying flat, then rolled atop her, so their bodies pressed together from chest to toes. He felt so good, warm and hard and wanting. "It's been so long since I've been with anyone who really mattered to me," he said, his breath tickling her neck near the sensitive spot just below her earlobe, making her shiver. "I feel like I know you so well, Kelsey. It's like coming home."

Touched, her chest ached with something new. Not love exactly, but perhaps love-adjacent. She'd known Ryan Ward for nearly half of her life, had a secret crush on him nearly as long. And now he was here, touching her, kissing her, making her want him inside her. Deep, deep, inside her.

"It makes it hotter, yeah?" she said, smiling up at him after she'd tugged his T-shirt off, running her hands over all the ridges and planes of his toned, tanned torso. Man, she could just eat him right up. Maybe she would too, before the night was over.

"Yeah," he panted, undoing the buttons on her blouse and easing it off her between kisses and nuzzles, then taking off her bra as well, before bending to take one of her taut nipples into his mouth. Kelsey cried out and arched against him. Good. So good. Then he pulled away, leaving her wanting more. "I need to make this good for you, Kelsey."

"Oh, it's gonna be good." Then she pulled him down again for another hot, opened-mouthed kiss. His mouth moved over hers, soft and warm and infinitely inviting, and she hauled him closer between her thighs, deepening their kiss.

Kelsey gasped and Ryan took advantage, sliding his tongue into her mouth to slide and dance with hers. She wasn't sure she'd ever get enough. His hand tangled in the hair at the nape of her neck, angling her head and keeping her close, as if he feared she'd disappear.

When they finally broke apart again, he rested his forehead against hers, their heavy breaths mingling in the small space between them. He looked deep into her eyes and asked, "Are you sure this is what you want, Kelsey?"

In answer, she slid her hands up his chest and around his neck, savoring his answering shiver. "More than anything."

"Okay." His answering grin made her inside go molten. Especially the way he whispered that word, all low and gruff and alpha as he rubbed his chest against her bare breasts, making her cry out from pleasure. She wrapped her legs around his waist, holding him right where he was, right where she needed him most. Hands seemed to be everywhere at once—touching, stroking, undoing, removing the rest of their clothes.

"You are so beautiful," Ryan said, his tone reverent, once they were both naked. He leaned over her, his weight resting on one elbow as he traced his fingertips down the center of her chest, between her breasts, over her quivering stomach, all the way down to the slick heat between her legs. With a shaky moan, Kelsey parted her thighs for him and sighed at the first touch of his long, talented fingers against her tender folds. "That's it, baby," Ryan coaxed, watching her as he played with her. "Let me see your passion, let me see you come apart for me."

Kelsey pulled him down for another heated kiss as she ground herself against his hand. He inserted first one, then two fingers inside her, spreading her wetness, getting her body ready to accommodate him. His thumb gently circled her most sensitive flesh and soon, she teetered on the edge of climax.

Ryan bent and took one of her taut nipples into his mouth again, sucking before grazing the sensitive peak gently with his teeth. The added sensation was enough to send her spiraling over the edge. Every muscle in her body clenched and Kelsey bit back a joyous scream of release as she rode out wave after wave of exquisite pleasure. He continued to stroke and coax her through her orgasm, teasing out every single last bit of sensation for her until she rested limply in his arms, sated.

Smiling, Kelsey slid her hand down his torso to take his hard cock in hand. "Your turn."

"No, baby," he said, but she refused to listen, pushing him over onto his back on the sofa, then straddling his thighs once more. He was bigger and stronger than her and could easily have pushed her off, but she knew what he really wanted, what he really needed. Bending over him, she kissed a slow trail down his muscled chest, stopping to admire the SEAL team tattoo on his left pec before teasing his small brown nipples with her nails, rubbing and flicking them through the light smattering of dark hair.

Kelsey continued her erotic trek down the ridges of his taut stomach, stopping to kiss each of his hip bones before tracing her tongue down those muscles that formed a delicious V all the way to his hard cock. He was big and so ready, a pearl of moisture glistening on his tip. Staring up into his pretty green eyes, she licked him, taking that salty drop into her mouth, savoring his flavor. His nostrils flared as crimson dotted his high cheekbones and his fingers tightened slightly against her scalp—not enough to hurt, but enough to make her pleasantly certain that she was straining his self-control.

"Like that?" she teased, licking him again, this time for root to tip, spending a bit of extra time on that sensitive spot behind his crown.

He groaned low and rough, gritting out his response. "Fuck, yes! Please, baby."

"Please what?" Kelsey took him into her mouth and sucked him deep. He thrust gently against the roof of her mouth and closed his eyes, his head tipping back and his expression pure ecstasy. She didn't think she'd ever seen a sexier sight in her life. "Tell me."

She released him from her mouth with an audible "pop", then grinned up at him.

Within seconds, Ryan had grasped her by the waist and rolled her beneath him once more, putting him firmly back in charge again. He reached over, grabbed his jeans from the floor and pulled out a condom from his back pocket, putting it on before covering her body with his again.

"Ready?" he asked as she raised her legs on either side of him, spreading her thighs farther to position him at her wet entrance. "God, I want you so bad right now."

"Then take me," she said.

He did, in one long thrust, burying himself hilt deep inside her. Kelsey bit back a gasp. It had been so long that it took a moment for her body to adjust to the size of him. But soon, her muscles relaxed and they found their rhythm. She met him stroke for stroke, urging him onward.

Ryan held himself above her, his arms shaking with the effort of holding himself back, his face sweaty, his cheeks ruddy with passion. She'd never seen him look more intense or more beautiful. She reached up and pushed his damp hair off his forehead.

"Okay?" he asked, even now concerned for her.

Touched by his kindness and attentiveness, Kelsey nodded, her breath catching as he hit just the right spot inside her. "Yes. God, yes. Right there. More, please. More."

"Always." He thrust harder and deeper inside her, angling himself to hit that spot again and again. Sensation sparked bright through her bloodstream, made stronger when he reached between them to stroke her throbbing folds again. Soon, she was heading straight for another climax.

"Are you close, baby?" Ryan asked, his breath panting and his eyes emerald bright.

"Yes. So close."

"Good." He drove her higher toward orgasm, his thrusts becoming faster and less controlled until finally her world shattered into nothing but light and heat and emotion. Ryan went still and stiff against her, his back arched and his head thrown back as he groaned loudly and came hard inside her. Together they clung to each other as they rode out the waves of their passion until, at last, their bodies calmed.

Ryan sank down onto the sofa beside her and pulled her into his arms, snuggling Kelsey into his side. Now that the heat of passion was over, she shivered, her sweat-slicked body chilled in the afterglow of great sex. She knew she could solve that problem by getting up and getting dressed, but lying there in his arms while he traced lazy patterns up and down her back with his fingers felt too good to give up just yet.

"God, I needed that," he said, his voice gravelly with exhaustion. "Are you okay, Kelsey?" he asked. "Was it good for you?"

"So good. You were wonderful." She laid her head on his chest and rested her hand over his heart. "I needed that too."

He kissed the top of her head. "We can work on the case again later. Together."

As Kelsey drifted off to sleep, she couldn't help smiling. Because after all, he was right. They would get through the case later and finish the last piece of the puzzle for his dad.

Together.

9

———————

Kelsey wasn't sure how long they dozed on her sofa, but the buzzing of her phone woke her up. She got up to answer, careful not to wake a still sleeping Ryan as she padded down the hall to her bedroom to grab her robe. "Hello?"

"Honey, is this a bad time?" her mother said. Kelsey winced. This was what she got for not checking the caller ID. Dammit. Normally, she loved talking to her mom—but talking to her while still naked, right after leaving her lover's arms, had the effect of making her feel like she was back in high school, getting caught necking on the couch with her boyfriend.

She tugged on her robe while her mom kept talking. "I heard from my friend Doreen at the grocery store that you're dating one of the Ward boys. Is that true?" Kelsey opened her mouth to answer, but didn't get the chance. "Because if it is, then I want to have you and whatever Ward boy it is over to dinner."

Oh Lord. There went the rest of her afterglow buzz.

Her parents were great—amazing, really. And since Amy, a fellow Marshal at the field office who'd been Kelsey's best friend, had moved to Phoenix to take a new position with the department, her mother was basically Kelsey's best friend. Both of her parents had been there for her through thick and thin. All the break-ups, all the training to become a Marshal. All the times when she'd doubted herself and needed a boost. The weekly dinners they shared were some of the best times of her week—a chance to recharge her batteries and revel in the fact she was loved, just as she was, with no disclaimers or unfair expectations. But because they loved their daughter so much, her parents tended to be overprotective. Kelsey was sure her mother meant well, inviting them over for dinner, but she suspected that it was also a chance for them to set Ryan straight on a few things.

Her parents could hold quite a grudge if they thought anyone had upset or mistreated their beloved daughter. And Ryan...well, Ryan hadn't mistreated her, exactly, but their high school rivalry had resulted in a whole slew of rants from her over dinner about how terrible, horrible, no good, and detestable he was.

As her mother, Lucette, continued to ramble on about something her father, Harold, had done, Kelsey hazarded a glance at Ryan. He was watching her with a look of... not distrust exactly, but wariness for sure. Yeah, she needed to nip this in the bud right now. The last thing she wanted was to take Ryan to dinner with her parents and have him get lectured through the entire meal about how he'd basically ruined Kelsey's life back in high school. Because while she could look back now and see that some of her rants against him might have been a little over the top, there was no denying that he'd been a genuine pain in the ass all through her high school career.

She and Ryan had had a kind of love-hate relationship, which had escalated quickly into a prank war. The jokes had started out fairly small. A whispered comment during class that made everyone laugh, or writing something on the chalkboard so that when the teacher moved the whiteboard, everyone would see it, like "Ryan Ward can't make a shot to save his life" or "Kelsey Poppins could get lost in a wet paper bag". And yeah, that last one was true. Her sense of direction, like her lying, was non-existent. So she'd worked hard to compensate, making sure she always knew where she was going ahead of time, being obsessed with physical maps, so in case her GPS went out or she lost her phone, she had a back-up. Kelsey loved maps.

But once the novelty of those smaller pranks wore off and they were no longer getting each other's attention with them, they moved on to bigger things, until the pranks culminated with the day that Ryan had filled her locker with marbles. In truth, Kelsey had been kind of impressed. And flattered, that he would put in that much time and effort. Because looking back now, it was obvious they'd both liked each other, but hadn't been ready to pursue those feelings. At the time, though, the marbles had gone everywhere and Kelsey hadn't looked before she'd stepped back and her foot slipped, causing her to fall awkwardly and break her arm. Everybody had seen it. And it was embarrassing, sure. Ryan got in big trouble for it too, nearly getting suspended from ROTC when it turned out he'd blown off drills to complete the prank. For a guy who loved the military, that was huge. Her arm had hurt like hell too. But what hurt even more was the fact that Ryan—after an earnest, shamefaced apology—had avoided her after that. That was when she knew her feelings for him had gone overboard from a crush to more, and she had to pull back. So she'd done her best to get over him, put him out of her mind.

Which led to the ill-fated fling with the basketball jock. She'd thought it was going pretty well, until prom. The jock had asked her, of course, but then she'd beaten him in a silly "battle of the sexes" basketball game during spirit week, and that had not gone over well. Kelsey was a competitive person, always had been, and she was good at shooting three-pointers. Except the jock didn't appreciate being shown up by his girlfriend, fragile asshole that he'd been, and so he'd broken up with her right after, cancelling their prom plans. Kelsey had slumped down on the now-empty bleachers and cried, looking up only once to find Ryan standing off to the side, watching her. He never said a word, though.

Kelsey had been crushed. Her parents, too. They'd met for the first time at their prom, so the idea of her having a perfect prom was almost as important to them as it had been for her. She'd bought the most gorgeous dress. Her parents had encouraged her to find a new date, but by then, no one was available since it was only a week away. Stupid Jack the Jock and his enormous ego ruined it all. She'd moped around school that week, thinking that was that. The only thing that cheered her up was hearing about the "sports war" that the boys had had—apparently at Ryan's suggestion. Somehow, Ryan had made a "mistake" and smacked asshole Jack right in the face with a basketball, breaking his nose. So much for looking like a prom king the next night. Bruised and battered, Jack had ended up missing the prom too. Though everyone treated it like an accident, Kelsey knew the truth. Ryan had avenged her. It had made her crush spring back even harder —which had her working overtime to suppress it, reminding herself at every opportunity how much Ryan Ward annoyed her. The annoying prankster Ryan Ward was the one she focused on, as a matter of self-preservation, until she nearly forgot the other Ryan Ward—the one who avenged her—even existed.

Until the day Ryan had shown back up in her life and swept her off her feet. Literally, in the case of the kiss in her office.

So yeah. No way was she taking him to her parents' house. And for the sake of her sanity, she should probably get a handle on her deepening emotions toward him before they started that freefall again. She'd learned her lesson about romance—she could be compatible with a man on *some* levels but not on all of them. And that was why love never worked out for her. She wasn't sure where the disconnect would happen with Ryan, but they'd get there eventually. If she was smart, she'd guard her heart until then, to keep it from hurting too badly when it all fell apart.

"Mom," she said, finally getting a word in edgewise. "I'm not dating him, okay? We're just pretending to be a couple for an undercover case we're working on together. That's all."

Of course, that wasn't exactly true anymore. Not after what had just happened between them on the sofa. Then again, she wasn't really sure what to call what they were, so it was hard to explain. And she really didn't want to, either, because this couldn't last, right? What was that old saying? The hotter the flame, the quicker it burns out? Yeah. That. She and Ryan had been playing with fire for a long time and now it was raging. Too hot, too much, too tempting to resist.

Her old nemesis reared its ugly head again, though. She couldn't lie. Had never been able to, and damn if her mother didn't pick up on it, just like she always did. "Kelsey Poppins, don't you even try to lie to me. You know I can always tell."

Sighing, Kelsey tried again. "Okay, fine. Things between Ryan and me are a little more complicated than that, but I'm still not sure exactly what it is we're doing together, so I don't want to label it yet, okay?"

Inside her, emotions pinged around like pinballs, fluctuating between happy and freaked out. The sex with Ryan had been amazing, the best she'd ever had with anyone. Their chemistry was off the frigging charts. But that didn't necessarily translate into a relationship.

Luckily, before her mother could ask any more questions that forced Kelsey to delve deeper into her feelings for Ryan, her phone buzzed with another call coming in. She checked her screen and saw that it was from the Marshal personnel office. She clicked back on with her mother. "Sorry, mom. I've got a work call on the other line. I'll call you back later about dinner. Bye."

Kelsey hung up before her mother had a chance to say anything else, then picked up the other line. "Marshal Poppins."

"This is Darcy, from the personnel office. You left a message."

Her heart tripped. "Oh, yes. Hi. Did you find anything out for me?"

"I did," the woman said, all business. "I was able to track down Kenny Burk's current position—and now I know why it wasn't easy to access that information in his records. He's finished doing under-cover work and is actually with Internal Affairs now. That department tends to require an extra level of discretion."

"I...I see." Kelsey glanced up and saw Ryan in the doorway in his jeans and nothing else. He frowned at her and she patted the bed beside her. He came over and took a seat next to her. "It's Internal Affairs," she whispered. "Apparently, Kenny Burk works there now."

Ryan's what-the-fuck expression matched exactly how Kelsey felt. She cleared her throat and asked, "How long has he been with that department?"

"About three months."

"Okay, then," Kelsey said, doing her best to keep her voice steady. If Kenny Burk was in IA, then that meant he'd have access to all the information she and Ryan had turned over when they'd passed off the investigation. She swallowed hard. "Thank you so much for checking into it for me."

She ended the call, then blinked at Ryan. "What the hell do we do now?"

"Well," he said, huffing out a breath. "What we *don't* do is trust anyone in Internal Affairs until we figure this out and solve the case. Looks like we're on our own."

"Oh God." Kelsey covered her face with her hands. Ryan put his arm around her shoulders and tugged her into his side. His warmth was comforting, but she still felt like the ground was crumbling beneath her. "This is such a mess. And what about what happened today? Someone tried to kill us, Ryan. *Again.*"

"I know." He buried his face in her hair and sighed. "But we still have each other to count on. And my brothers will help too, I'm sure." Ryan chuckled. "You're not ready to quit on me now, are you?"

She raised her head to glare at him. "Hell no. I'm not a quitter. Been there, done that, ain't going back."

"Wait." His brows knit. "You almost quit? I don't believe it."

"Yep. Nearly stopped being a Marshal because of a guy." She wrinkled her nose. "Longest twenty-four hours of my life. Definite low point. But it taught me that I never, ever want to go there again."

"That's my Kelsey." He kissed her cheek and snuggled her close.

Kelsey buried her face in his throat. She'd thought the sex had deepened their connection, she just hadn't realized how much until now. It was terrifying and thrilling. And while it might also be temporary, that didn't mean she couldn't enjoy it while it lasted, right?

10

The next morning, Ryan woke up next to Kelsey in her bed. They'd showered, made dinner in her apartment, watched a movie, then gone to bed early and made love again. It all felt so comfortable and cozy that he'd slept like a rock and had woken up in a great mood. In fact, he hadn't felt this relaxed and secure since… well, since he'd been a kid, actually.

On paper, his childhood probably sounded a little messed up. His dad had been married to the love of his life, but when he'd lost her to breast cancer when Lance was ten years old and Neal was three, he'd kind of fallen apart. Maybe some would condemn him for not buckling down to take care of his family, but from all reports, it had been all he could do to hold himself together. He'd thrown himself into work, first and foremost. And he'd thrown himself into some romantic relationships that hadn't meant much to him, just to try to fill the void. He hadn't been in love with Ryan's mom…but he *had* gotten her pregnant, and had then felt obligated to do the responsible thing by marrying her. The marriage hadn't lasted long, and she'd walked out when Ryan was four. He hadn't seen her since and only vaguely remembered her at all.

And yet despite all that, Ryan had never really felt deprived in any way. His two older brothers had seen to that. They'd never treated him any differently because he was a half-brother. They had always made him feel equal and loved and safe. Lance was basically his parent in every way that counted. He was the one who had packed a lunch for him for school, and read him bedtime stories, and helped him with his homework. He was the example Ryan had always wanted to follow—so when Lance joined ROTC and then the navy and then became a SEAL, that automatically became what Ryan wanted to do, too. Neal, closer in age to him, had been more like a traditional brother: teasing him, defending him, counseling him through crushes and broken hearts, teaching him how to throw a basketball, throw a punch, throw a party that wouldn't get broken up by the cops.

They'd been everything Ryan had needed to feel safe and loved—which was maybe why it was easier for him to build a good relationship with their father than it had been for his brothers. Ryan's expectations had been lower. He'd been fine with meeting the man where he was, rather than expecting him to suddenly turn around and become the attentive family man he'd apparently been before his first wife's death. The Gary Ward he knew had always been kind of a mess. Smart and savvy and honorable, but a mess, all the same.

Like father, like son, Ryan thought with a rueful smile. There was a certain irony in the idea that Gary's death had sent Ryan off the rails just like his first wife's death had done to Gary. The question was, would he go wandering through life, never really getting back on the right path, like his father had, or would he find a new way for himself now that the life he'd wanted had been turned upside down?

That was the question he found himself pondering as he wandered out to the kitchen to make breakfast for both of them. As he stirred up some eggs to scramble, he heard Kelsey in the shower and began to whistle to himself. After pouring the eggs into a pan and starting some bacon and toast to go with them, he picked up his phone from her spare charger and checked his emails.

An old SEAL team buddy of his had sent him a message with a potential job offer. Apparently the guy had started a paramilitary group that specialized in high-stakes hostage rescue situations around the world. From what his friend said, it sounded like most of their business came from rich people whose family members had been kidnapped and held for ransom in countries where kidnapping had become something of an industry in itself, like Mexico, Ecuador, and Brazil. But they also did the occasional rescue at the behest of governments when their citizens were being held by a foreign power but the government couldn't risk their own soldiers on the extraction for political reasons.

That sort of work played right into his skill set, honestly. He'd done a lot of similar work as a SEAL—including that ill-fated final mission to save those medical aid workers. It all sounded like a good fit, except for one caveat—you never knew when a mission would come in, how long it would last, or where it would take you. You had to be ready to go at the drop of a hat and you could never count on being home for birthdays or holidays. It was the kind of job that would have to come first in his life, the same way that being a SEAL had.

Ryan stirred the eggs in the pan with a spatula, frowning. If he'd gotten that email before he'd gotten involved with Kelsey, it would have been the perfect offer for him. Now, he wasn't so sure. Yesterday, nearly dying in that apartment building, he'd been reminded of how much of his life he'd kept on hold, just assuming he'd have time for it later. Maybe he was finally ready for that "later." But he still wasn't certain. Either way, he'd keep the email, keep thinking about the offer. He couldn't make such a big decision about his future just based on where things *might* go with Kelsey. Yes, they'd had sex. Yes, it had been amazing. But did that mean it could grow into something more? He wasn't sure.

His own relationship history wasn't great. After all the stuff with Kelsey in high school, he'd tried dating someone else for a while. A cheerleader named Brittany. It had been fun, the sex had been amazing, and they'd remained good friends. But the romance? Yeah, that fizzled pretty fast. Over the years since then, he'd hooked up a lot and also had a few friends-with-benefits situations during his time in the SEALs, but never any real relationships. It just didn't make sense for that stage of his life. And honestly, he'd never met a woman he cared about enough to rethink his old opinion that you could only focus on one thing at a time. He knew that people liked to say that you could "have it all," but something still had to come first. For him, it had always been the work. Was he ready to put something else in that number one slot? And if he did decide to focus on his personal life for a change, what kind of job could he have that wouldn't take over his life? What kind of job was he even qualified for, after only ever being a military man?

What kind of job would he look for if he stayed in Detroit? He and Kelsey worked pretty well together, but once they'd solved things, she'd go back to being a Marshal and he'd... what? He supposed he could go work at the agency, with his brothers. He definitely liked investigating cases. But before he could ask his brothers to hire him on, he'd have to explain the real reason he left his SEAL team, and then deal with their judgment and disappointment about it, and damn. He just wasn't ready to face that yet.

Kelsey wandered in and slipped her arms around his waist to hug him from behind, looking around his arm to see what he was doing. "What are you reading on your phone?"

"Oh, uh..." He quickly closed the email, then set his phone aside to turn and kiss her. "Just checking my emails is all." She didn't need to know about the job offer until he'd decided. "Got one from an old SEAL buddy. He heard I was out of the military now and all."

"That's nice." She rose on tiptoes to kiss him again, then sniffed the air. "Breakfast smells good."

"It is." He grinned and plopped a couple slices of American cheese atop the eggs, then stirred them in before turning off the burner. "Want to grab some plates? This is done."

"Sure."

He served up their food and they took a seat at the breakfast bar to eat. Ryan was eager to change the subject to something other than that email, but she beat him to it when she checked her watch. "I need to get to the office soon. Don't want to be late."

"Finish your breakfast, then I'll drive you," he said, shoveling in more eggs. In the military, you had to eat fast because you never knew when you were going to get called out again. It was a habit that had stuck, unfortunately. "I think while you're at the office, I'm going to go back to that apartment building and talk to some of the surrounding places. See if anyone has any surveillance footage from yesterday, like we talked about. Then maybe I'll see if I can figure out who some of the previous tenants were, check for connections with Kenny Burk or another Marshal."

"I think that sounds like a great idea," Kelsey said, gobbling down her last few bites of food before giving him another quick kiss. "Okay, let's go. Oh, my mom wants us to come over for dinner tonight. I told her we'd be there. Is that all right?"

Ryan nodded. "Sounds good."

～

Dinner that night at Kelsey's parents' house was great, actually. They sat around talking and reminiscing about stuff from the past while they

83

ate pot roast and potatoes. Her parents were a little wary of him at first, bringing up some of his more notable high school pranks in a way that made it clear they weren't sure whether or not they should hold a grudge, but he'd turned up the charm and had eventually won them over—especially by bringing up some of the especially epic pranks Kelsey had played on *him* in return. They hadn't heard those stories before. It was nice, talking about that stuff, some of which he'd nearly forgotten entirely. But it also reminded Ryan about how strange it felt to operate in the civilian world again. He felt a bit out of place, removed from it all, like he was in a foreign land and learning the customs.

Of course, he was already feeling a bit unsettled because his investigations that day hadn't really panned out. He hadn't gotten hold of any surveillance footage, though a couple people said they'd get back to him. He hadn't had much luck tracking down information about the building's former tenants, either. All in all, it felt like he hadn't gotten much done with his day.

As they were finishing up with her mom and Kelsey was saying her goodbyes, Ryan checked his phone and found that one of the people he'd asked about surveillance footage earlier in the day had called back, saying that he had something Ryan might want to see.

Once they were outside, Ryan handed Kelsey the keys. "I need to make a call. Go ahead and get in and start the car so you don't get cold."

He hit redial on the number and waited for them to answer.

"Jet's Auto Body and Towing."

"Hi, this is Ryan Ward, returning your call," he said, shuffling slightly next to the car to keep warm. Well, that, and to disperse some of his nervous energy. They could really use a bit of good news on the case front. "You said you found something in the surveillance footage?"

Please say you found something.

"Oh yeah," the guy said. "I think I might have."

Ryan avoided doing a fist pump, barely. "Great. Can I swing by now and take a look at it?"

"Sorry, man. Can't now. Shop's closed and I just got an emergency call for a tow across town for an accident. Could take a while. Call me back tomorrow and we'll set something up."

Well, fuck. He sighed, his breath frosting on the chilly air. "Okay. Will do. Thanks."

It wasn't the break he'd hoped for, but it was something.

He said as much to Kelsey as he climbed inside the car, warm air from the vents blasting him.

"Well, it's not like we could've done much with it tonight anyway," she said, shrugging.

He fastened his seatbelt, frowning. "Yeah, I guess."

But in his mind, he felt stymied, like he was letting his dad down somehow by not going full throttle on this thing. Which was silly. His dad wouldn't want him running himself into the ground. *Work smarter, not harder* was always his dad's motto. Ryan exhaled slowly and headed back toward Kelsey's place. He couldn't help remembering how squirrelly the guy with the surveillance footage had acted when Ryan had first called him. Would he be that bad again tomorrow? Would he decide against sharing the surveillance footage after all? What if tonight was Ryan's best shot to get the information, and he'd blown it?

He signaled and turned the corner, cursing himself. If only he'd stayed home and focused on the case instead of trying to impress the parents of the woman he was sleeping with, maybe he could have talked to that guy and gotten in to see the footage before he closed for the day. But no. Instead, he'd prioritized the personal over the professional, and as a result he'd made Kelsey happy, but he'd missed out on the chance to close the case that was putting her in harm's way. Now, Ryan had to continue to worry about solving the final piece of the puzzle of his dad's murder and keep Kelsey safe in the process. Not good. Not good at all.

11

The next day, after she got off work, Kelsey and Ryan drove over to Ward Investigation. Even though she was loath to admit it, she felt nervous. This would be the first time she was meeting Ryan's soon-to-be sister-in-law, Lori, and it would also be her first visit to the family's PI offices. It wasn't exactly a typical meet-the-family situation, but it had her on edge all the same. Her anxiety wasn't helped by the weird vibes Ryan had been giving off since they'd had dinner with her parents last night. He seemed tense and a little distant, and she wasn't quite sure why. As far as Kelsey could tell, things had gone well. Ryan had been charming and while her parents could be a lot sometimes, they'd gotten along great, once they'd moved past the initial awkwardness. So, what was it?

Distracted, she tried to talk about something else besides her own muddled feelings. "Did you have a chance to look at the security tape you got from that business owner near the apartment building?"

"Yep," Ryan said, checking his rearview mirror before changing lanes. "Unfortunately, there wasn't anything incriminating that I noticed. I did still record the license plates of any cars that passed by the area in and around the time we were there, just in case. I'm hoping Lori will agree to run them through the system for me. We'll see if anything comes of that."

A few minutes later, they pulled up in front of a newly renovated downtown storefront. A discreet gold plaque set into the granite proclaimed Ward Investigation. Ryan parked at the curb and they got out. Kelsey remembered hearing something on the news about the city's efforts to revitalize this area, and from what she could see, they'd succeeded. It was cool that Ryan and his family had been a part of that.

They walked inside the offices, Ryan holding the door for her, and Kelsey took a deep, calming breath, noting that the air was still scented with fresh paint and lemon floor wax—sort of the building equivalent of a "new car" smell. The hardwood beneath her feet gleamed beneath the recessed overhead lighting, and soft instrumental music played over the sound system. From the comfortable, stylish yet functional furniture to the local artists' paintings on the wall, the place felt more like a posh consulting office than the cluttered, dusty, somewhat rundown *film noir* vibe she'd been expecting from a private investigation agency. Maybe she'd watched too many Humphrey Bogart movies.

Before she could think about it too long, a pretty woman with curly auburn hair walked over, smiling. "Hey, Ryan. We've been waiting for you."

"Sorry we're late. Traffic," Ryan said, pulling the slim woman in for a hug. When they pulled back, he kept his arm around her shoulders, grinning. "Kelsey, this is my soon-to-be sister-in-law and Neal's part-ner, Lori Hart. Lori, this is Kelsey Poppins. She's the US Marshal who is helping me with Dad's case."

"So nice to meet you at last," Lori said, shaking Kelsey's hand, her smile broad and genuine. "Ryan's told us a lot about you."

"He has?" Kelsey asked, her surprised gaze darting to Ryan as heat prickled her cheeks. She felt both thrilled and terrified by that prospect. "Good things, I hope."

"Of course." Lori laughed, elbowing Ryan gently in the ribs, making him move away slightly and drop his arm to his side. "Well, as good as Ryan gets, anyway. Sometimes getting info out of this guy is like cracking a safe. You ask him a question, and after fifteen more minutes of conversation, you realize he somehow managed to avoid ever answering it."

"Agreed." Kelsey felt a bit of the tension inside her release. Lori seemed friendly and nice. And it was kind of fun to have someone to commiserate over a Ward man with. She followed him and Lori to a neat desk near the back corner of the open space. "Your office is lovely."

"Thank you!" Lori took a seat behind her desk and Ryan and Kelsey sat in comfy chairs in front of it. "I loved our old office, of course, but Gary was never really one to make updates—more of an 'if it ain't broke, don't fix it' type. It ended up giving the office kind of a…retro feel," she said, leaving Kelsey to wonder if what she'd initially imagined had been pretty on target after all. "But of course, we needed a whole new setup after the fire, and it felt like a good opportunity to try out a new vibe in our new location. Neal gave me crap over the cost of some of this stuff, but I held firm. We want our clients to feel relaxed and safe when they come here. They're already stressed over having to hire a PI in the first place, so an inviting environment will hopefully help get people in the door and build our business even faster."

"Just as long as you don't get so busy that you no longer have time to do favors for your favorite soon-to-be little brother," Ryan teased.

Lori laughed. "I think I can manage to squeeze you into my busy schedule. Do you have the security camera footage for me?" Ryan had thought it wouldn't hurt to get a second opinion and Kelsey agreed. While Ryan had a fair amount of experience in PI work thanks to his dad, or so he'd said, Lori's experience was a lot more recent. She might pick up on something the two of them had missed.

"I do." Ryan pulled out his phone and tapped the screen, then set it aside on the desk. "Just sent the file to your secure email."

"Great." Lori swiveled slightly in her chair to face her computer and pulled up the footage. "Let's see what we've got."

"Thanks," he said, standing to walk around the desk and lean over Lori's shoulder to go over the footage with her.

Kelsey chimed in where she could, but eventually sat back in her chair while they went over the footage minute by minute. A few minutes passed as she checked her own emails. When she glanced up, she noticed Ryan's phone vibrating on the desktop. He was still engrossed in the security footage with Lori, so she picked it up, intending to pass it to him to answer. But instead of a call coming in, the screen was filled with a flurry of text messages from someone called SEAL914. And while she didn't mean to be a snoop, it was hard not to read at least a few of them before she shut it off.

Apparently, there was some kind of job offer involved and SEAL914 wanted to know if Ryan wanted it or not. She set the phone back down and waited for a break in the conversation between him and Lori to say, "Uh, Ryan. Your friend keeps texting you. Something about a job, and whether you're interested in it? Want to tell me about that?"

"Oh, right." Ryan straightened and rubbed the back of his neck, his expression visibly uncomfortable. "He owns a private security firm dealing with hostage rescue. He thinks I might be a great fit for his company now that I'm done with the SEALs."

"Wow," Lori said. "That actually does sound like a good fit for you, Ry." She smiled at Kelsey. "Don't you think?"

"Sure," Kelsey said, frowning down at her hands, then glancing back up at Lori. "Sounds great."

Lori's smile faltered, her gaze darting between Ryan and Kelsey, but she didn't say anything.

Ryan hesitated a second, like he wanted to say more, but then he just sighed and picked up his phone. "I need to reply so he'll stop blowing up my phone. Be right back."

Kelsey sat staring at her shoes as the cheerful chime above the door went off at Ryan's exit. She'd thought after last night, they weren't keeping secrets from each other anymore, but she'd been wrong.

"Hey," Lori said, her tone concerned. "Everything okay?"

"Yep, fine." More from habit than anything, Kelsey nodded fast, forcing a smile as she focused on Lori again. "And you're right. That job does sound perfect for Ryan's skillset. Obviously."

"Sure." Lori sat back, arms crossed, narrowing her gaze on Kelsey like a laser. "But you didn't know about it, did you?"

Kelsey blinked at her a second before sighing. This was what happened when your face was an open book—especially around a woman who was perceptive for a living. It seemed there was no point in being anything but honest, since Lori would obviously know the truth either way. So Kelsey shook her head. "No. I found out just now when I picked up his phone." She shrugged. "I guess it bothers me he didn't tell me about it."

"I see." Lori gave her an empathetic look. "You guys are together, aren't you?"

"Oh, uh…" Kelsey opened her mouth, closed it, then opened it again, unsure what to say. But she'd kept all this in so long, her resistance crumbled. It would be so nice to have someone to talk to about all the confusing emotions inside her, and Lori seemed so understanding and trustworthy. And she was engaged to a Ward brother, which meant she knew how they thought. In the end, Kelsey went for it. "Yeah, we are. It started out as a fake relationship for the sake of the case, but now it's all too real." She huffed out a breath and sank back in her seat. "Not that it matters, though, because if he takes a job like that, then we probably wouldn't be able to sustain a relationship long-term. I've had issues before because my job is so demanding and calls for a lot of travel. I can't imagine how a relationship would work with *two* people with unpredictable schedules. When would we ever see each other?"

"Hmm." Lori seemed to consider that a moment, then sat forward. "Are you busy tonight?"

She thought about it. She'd assumed that she and Ryan would go back to her place and make dinner, maybe watch a movie or something. Nothing big, just a quiet night in like they'd had two nights ago. It had sounded good to her a minute ago, but right now, she was thinking she could use a little break from him, to clear her head. "No, actually. I'm not."

"Great." Lori grinned broadly. "Then come to dinner with me." She lowered her voice for just Kelsey to hear. "Listen, the Ward brothers are wonderful, but believe me. I know that being with one of them can be… challenging sometimes. Especially when you're working a case together. So yeah. Come out with me. Blow off some steam and have a nice evening. How 'bout it?"

Kelsey found herself smiling too. "I'd like that. Thank you."

The chimes above the door went off again as Ryan re-entered the office and they finished going through the footage. Once they were done, Ryan stood and stretched.

"Ready to go?" he asked Kelsey.

"Um, actually, you go on ahead," she told him, pushing to her feet. "Lori and I are going to grab dinner together."

He looked satisfyingly disappointed. *Good,* she thought. Let him miss her a little bit.

"Yep." Lori stood too. "If you need something to keep yourself busy tonight, Ry, Neal's on a stakeout for one of our clients. Go hang out with him. I'm sure he'd appreciate the company."

12

———————

Sitting in a cramped car with his brother was not where Ryan had pictured his day ending, yet here he was. He scooted a little in his seat to try to get more comfortable, accidentally knocking some empty candy wrappers and chip bags onto the floor. On stakeout, you had to eat what you could, when you could, and it needed to be something easily portable so that you could keep a constant eye on the target. So yeah. They had a lovely dinner of fast-food burgers, followed by vending machine snacks and drinks from the machines on the corner near the convenience store. It wasn't the worst he'd ever had, of course, but it sure as hell didn't hold a candle to the meal he'd thought he'd be sharing with Kelsey.

He hoped Kelsey's dinner with Lori was better. At the same time, he worried about what they might talk about together. Were they busy trash-talking him right now? Shit. He should have told her about that job offer upfront, but dammit, he had a lot on his mind, stuff he was still working through and—

"Mind telling me what the fuck your problem is, bro?" Neal said, giving him a look.

"What?" Ryan scrunched his nose. "I don't have a problem."

"Right. You just look like someone pooped on your parade for no reason, then. Great." He sighed and took another swig of his energy drink, grimacing at the taste. Ryan and Neal agreed that energy drinks were disgusting—but they were also necessary. You never knew how long stakeouts would last, so you had to stay alert. "Remind me to thank my almost-wife for sticking me with your sad-sack ass all night. And here I thought I was done babysitting you once you turned twelve or so."

Ryan gave that the response it deserved—a big old middle finger—then shook his head, falling back on his usual tactic of trying to get the focus off him. "What's this stakeout for again?"

Neal looked through his binoculars at the office building across the street again, then sat back, letting the things flop down against his chest. "Client thinks someone's been breaking in and stealing files. Based on everything Lori and I have worked out so far, we figure it has to be happening at night. So Lori and I have been taking turns watching the place for the last two nights. Nothing so far, but maybe it'll be lucky number three."

"Huh," Ryan grunted, shifting again. His ass was going numb.

"So we've got plenty of time for you to spit out whatever it is that has you so mopey, bro."

He really didn't like the thought of getting into it. But dammit. He needed someone to talk through all this shit with and Neal was the only one there, so… He sighed, skirting around his issues with Kelsey and picking up the smallest of his problems to start with. "I got a job offer and I'm trying to decide whether to take it or not."

"Job offer?" Neal gave him a look. "So you're definitely not going back to your team? I know you said you were leaving to focus on this investigation, but I wasn't sure if that meant you were planning on going back."

Fuck. He hadn't planned on getting into all that at all tonight, but then there really wasn't a good time to tell your family about a less-than-honorable discharge from the military, so he went for it.

"I can't go back."

"Can't?"

"Medical discharge," Ryan bit out. "For mental health. I've actually got my discharge hearing coming up—heard from my CO just the other day."

Neal didn't say anything, he just waited. Silently there for his little brother, just like always. That made it a little easier to force the words out.

"It was a hostage situation. Orders were to stay put—wait on the weather. I thought the hostages didn't have that long. I led the team in anyway. I was right, but I was also insubordinate. My CO tried to cut me a break, since I'd just learned that Dad had died before I made the decision to go in. Mental health discharge was the compromise. I knew before I even came home." It wasn't quite the level of detail he'd shared with Kelsey, but openness felt easier with her, maybe because she was always so transparently open herself. It felt safe to share anything with her.

To his credit, Neal listened to Ryan's tale without interrupting. When it was over, he just sat there, blinking out the windshield, his expression unreadable. For the first time in his life, Ryan felt nervous around his sibling, unsure of how Neal might react.

When a few more minutes ticked by, though, with no response from Neal, the silence grew too uncomfortable for Ryan to stand. "It's probably for the best," he said, trying to minimize the damage that had been done and his still-raging feelings over all of it. Ryan shrugged and stared out the window beside him because looking at his brother was too hard at that point, in case he saw disappointment there, or worse, pity. "I'm fine with it. Really. Gives me a clean break. Now I can move forward into my future, decide what I want to do from here. It's all good."

"It is not all good, bro," Neal said at last. But instead of his tone sounding judgmental, Neal's voice came across as caring and concerned. Ryan hazarded a glance at him as Neal reached over to clap him on the shoulder. "I'm sorry that happened to you, Ry— though I'm proud of you for saving those hostages."

Ryan shrugged again and looked out into the darkness beyond. He'd never been super comfortable being the center of attention, especially now. Neal knew him well enough to pick up on that, thankfully, and changed subjects.

His brother cleared his throat, then used his binoculars again to check the building across the way, saying, "What's holding you back from taking this job, then?"

"I don't know." *Liar.* Ryan knew damned well why he was hesitating. "I guess it's because of Kelsey." Admitting it out loud for the first time felt weird. And right. "We're together. For real now."

Neal gave him a silent stare.

"Yeah, I know. It started out fake, but then things happened and..." He frowned and rolled his eyes, making a vague gesture. "Anyway, the point is, I like what we have. It's good and easy. And honestly, I'm tired of living out of a suitcase and having nothing to care about except for the mission at this point. I really am ready to move on." Ryan scowled down at his hands in his lap, twisting a candy wrapper into a tight knot. "Or at least, I think I am. But what if it turns out I'm really *not* ready? What if I can't make the switch back to civilian life?

With Dad gone and my military career in the toilet in one fell swoop, I'm not sure I'm ready to commit to anything yet, you know? No matter how great things are with Kelsey now."

"Hmm." Neal fiddled with the buttons on the dashboard, adjusting the heat. "Well, if you want my vote, I say stay with Kelsey. A job is much easier to replace than a woman."

Ryan snorted. "I bet if you asked Lance, he'd say differently."

"Yeah?" Neal raised a brow at him and pulled out his phone. "I'll take that bet. One hundred bucks."

Shit. Maybe his brother was right, but he couldn't back down now. Pride was involved.

"Fine. Call him."

Neal gave a Cheshire cat grin as he hit speed dial, then put the call on speakerphone so they could both hear. It rang twice before it picked up.

"Ward," their older brother answered.

"Hey, dude," Neal said. "Ry and I have a little bet going you can decide. But first, our little bro wants to tell you the truth about what happened with his SEAL team."

Outraged, Ryan glared at his brother, but fuck. He was kind of trapped now, and since he'd told Neal it was only a matter of time until Lance found out about it too. Shit. Fine. He took a deep breath and relayed the story a third time, finding that at each retelling, it stung less and less. Finally, he ended with the new job offer he'd gotten and then the question that was the basis for their bet, about whether a job was more easily replaced than women. "What's your verdict?"

Lance remained quiet a moment and Ryan could picture the wheels turning in his brother's head, until at last Lance said, "Well, I think it would be great for all of us to stay in Detroit together."

Great. Lance was staying neutral as Switzerland. Same as always.

Not helpful at all.

"Come on," Ryan whined. "I've got a Benjamin on the line here. Give me something."

Lance huffed out a breath. "And why would I make it that easy for either one of you, hmm? I'm just saying, if you stayed in Detroit, then we could all work at the agency together. I'll be joining Lori and Neal in a few weeks when my retirement is finally official. You know there's a place for you, too, if you want it. But on the other hand, I also know what it's like to have a career you love, Ryan. And how sometimes that career takes you in a different direction from the woman you care about. It's never an easy choice to make but in the long run, going your separate ways might end up being the best thing that could happen to both of you. It might not be 'no' but rather 'not yet.' You'll end up where you're supposed to be when the time is right."

"Thanks, bro. That helps not at all," Neal grumbled. "You know, you're damned lucky Ruth didn't marry someone else while your stupid ass was away."

They bickered a bit while Ryan kept circling that thought in his head. Would that happen to him if he took the job? Would Kelsey end their relationship and end up marrying some other guy?

In that moment, it was a massive relief to look over and see that someone actually was breaking into the building. Finally, an excuse to end this damned conversation. He slapped Neal's arm and pointed over. "Check it out, bro. Third night's lucky after all."

"Fuck!" Neal fumbled for the phone. "Someone's breaking into the building. We need to go, Lance."

Neal ended the call as Ryan undid his seatbelt, his legs stiff as he climbed out of the passenger side of the car and pulled his service weapon from his waist holster, checking the safety. Neal did the same on his side of the car, and the two of them headed for the building about a half a block up, sticking to the shadows to avoid being seen.

In the end, it was an easy capture. The guy trying to get in was a total amateur and Neal and Ryan were able to sneak up on him with no problems at all. While Neal called it in, Ryan secured the guy's wrists with a zip tie he'd stashed in his jacket pocket earlier, just in case. The whole time, though, Ryan was preoccupied with the idea of Kelsey moving on to some other guy after he left to go off saving hostages in some foreign land.

13

A few days later, Ryan lay in bed with Kelsey. It was still early, pre-dawn based on the grayish light streaming in through the blinds on the window, but he couldn't go back to sleep. Kelsey was awake too, tracing lazy patterns on his chest with her fingers and making him shiver with delight because it felt so fucking good.

Ever since the other night at the Ward Investigation offices when she'd picked up his phone and seen those messages from his buddy about the job offer, they seemed to have reached some sort of fragile, unspoken truce. It worked as long as neither of them talked about the future.

Honestly, even though Ryan knew they were just kicking the can down the road and that eventually they'd have to deal with it, he was okay living in the fantasy a bit longer. When he took the time to really think about it and examine his feelings, it scared the living shit out of him how much he cared about Kelsey.

They lay there for a while, not talking, just enjoying the closeness of being together, while Ryan's mind drifted to his dad's case again. There still weren't any good new leads for them to follow, and he was going over every piece of information they'd received to see if there was anything they'd missed the first couple times around.

That was when something clicked in his head and he pushed himself up onto his elbows, dislodging Kelsey slightly from where she was draped over his chest.

"What's wrong?" she asked, frowning up at him.

"I just thought of something with the case." He scooted higher so his back rested against the headboard, the sheet slipping down to his hips. "Remember that day when we went to the prison and talked to that guard? He said he was new, that he'd replaced a guy who died in a drunk driving accident."

"Yeah, so?" Kelsey sat up too, yawning and rubbing her eyes with one hand while holding the sheet to her chest with the other. "What's that got to do with anything?"

"Well, hear me out." Adrenaline rushed through his system, chasing away any remaining traces of sleep from his brain. "What if it wasn't an accident after all? Remember the day your brakes were cut? We saw that empty vodka bottle in the backseat—it was what made me think your car had been tampered with, that someone wanted to make it look like you'd been driving drunk. What if you weren't the first person Burk tried that with? Maybe he thought he could get away with it because he'd already done so once before."

Facts and theories were popping into his head now at breakneck speed. Ryan got up and tugged on his sweatpants from the night before, then grabbed his laptop and sat on the edge of the bed. "I need to track down the information on that prison guard who died." He started with a Google search and when that didn't produce anything other than an obituary, he headed to social media instead. Amazing what kinds of personal stuff people posted on there. More than enough to get all the information on a guy if…

"Got it!" he said, grinning in the pre-dawn gloom. Kelsey scooted up behind him to peer over his shoulder at the screen. A photo of a newspaper article showed up on a relative's newsfeed, along with a plethora of comments from the bereaved friends and family. "See? I'll bet you my hunch is right."

Kelsey agreed with him. "Yep. It does look suspicious."

Ryan did a bit more searching and managed to find the account for the dead guard's widow. He took down her name, then searched the local property tax records to find her address. "We should go talk to her this morning," he said, kissing Kelsey quickly over his shoulder. "Unless you have other plans."

"Besides work, you mean?" She raised an auburn brow at him.

"Oh, right. Sorry. What time are you due in?" He sent the widow's info to the wireless printer, then shut his laptop.

"Nine. And I can't be late because Phil is riding my ass hard these days." She looked over at the clock on the nightstand, then back to him. "You'll just have to go interview her yourself, then let me know what you find."

"Damn." He kissed her over his shoulder again, then stood. "According to Google, it'll be an hour's drive outside the city. If we get ready now, we'll have time for breakfast together before I head over there." Since Kelsey had borrowed her mom's car until hers could be fixed, she no longer needed him to drop her off and pick her up from work. That meant he could head out as soon as they were done eating.

Then she stood too, letting the sheet fall away. His breath caught at the sight of her and he damned near chucked all their plans and took her back to bed immediately. But Kelsey was already on her way to the bathroom, stopping at the doorway and turning to beckon him with a finger. "There's room for two in here, you know."

She didn't have to ask him twice.

∼

Three hours later, Ryan sat in a cozy living room across from the prison guard's widow. She was a middle-aged woman named Julie with dark hair and darker circles under her eyes. Ryan imagined she must have been through hell the past year or so, dealing with the unexpected death of her husband and everything that followed. She'd just sent their kids off to school on the bus when he'd arrived, and he'd managed to catch her before she got ready for her own job at an accounting firm.

"Thanks so much for speaking with me this morning, Ms. Patrick," Ryan said, sipping from the cup of bitter coffee she'd gotten for them. "Once again, I'm very sorry for your loss." He cleared his throat. "I recently lost my father unexpectedly, so I know what you're going through." Ryan took a deep breath. "The reason I'm here is I'm investigating a case related to my father's death and had a few questions I hoped you might be able to answer."

Ryan handed the woman his phone with the image of Kenny Burk. It was an old office Christmas party photo that Kelsey had sent him, but Neal had zoomed in on Kenny so that his face filled the screen. "Do you ever remember seeing this man at all around your husband? Perhaps in the days just before October nineteenth of last year?"

Ms. Patrick frowned down at the image. "No, I'm sorry. He doesn't look familiar at all."

"Okay, thank you," Ryan said, doing his best not to sound as discouraged as he felt.

"But," the widow continued, "now that you mention it, there was a different man who came to the house not long before my husband's accident," she said. "I'm not sure of the date, but I think…" she pulled out her own phone, bringing up her calendar. "Yes, it was on October fourteenth, because I remember our son had a ballgame that night. My husband wasn't able to join us—he said he needed to stay overtime on a shift, but when we got home, he was here, talking with another man. He wasn't anyone I'd seen before." Ryan's SEAL instincts said they were on to something here. "He didn't look anything like that guy, though. The man who came to the house was medium height, balding, white. Maybe in his mid-forties."

Ryan blinked at her a moment, taking that in, his pulse kicking up several notches. "Did that man show a badge that you remember? One that said US Marshal's office?"

"No." Ms. Patrick shook her head. "Not that he showed me, anyway."

Throat tight, he adjusted the Christmas party photo on his phone, reframing it so that it was a zoomed in on Phil Johnson instead of Kenny Burk. "Was it this man?"

"Yep. That's him. Who is he?" the widow asked.

Just the boss of the woman I love.

He didn't say that, though. Instead, he swallowed hard and stuffed his phone back in his pocket, his mind racing. He had to get out of there. Had to call Kelsey and warn her. "Uh," Ryan said, standing. "Thank you so much for your time, Ms. Patrick. I really appreciate it."

Ryan barely made it to the curb where he'd parked before he called Kelsey.

"Where are you?" he asked as soon as she picked up.

"At my desk. Why?"

"Is anyone there in the office with you?"

"Just the intern and Phil. Everyone else is out on assignments for the rest of the day." He could hear her confusion through the phone line.

His blood ran cold at that last name she'd mentioned. "Ryan, you sound awful. What the hell is going on?"

Fuck.

The woman he loved was sitting in an office over an hour away with the man who had repeatedly tried to kill her. His first instinct was to warn her to get out of there ASAP, then get in his car and burn rubber back to her side. But Kelsey couldn't lie to save her life. Literally. So he didn't want to do anything that might alert Phil that they were on to him.

Then there was also the matter of the intern, who was also innocent, and could get hurt or worse in the crossfire. So no. He needed to handle this differently. He took a deep breath and thought through the outcomes, assessed the threat, as he'd been trained to do in the SEALs. Phil was unlikely to make a move in the office in front of a witness unless he had reason to suspect that Kelsey had somehow discovered the truth. Which meant Kelsey couldn't know the truth—not yet. Not while she was in harm's way.

"Nothing. Sorry. I'm just out of sorts, I guess." He glanced back at the house, then climbed behind the wheel of his vehicle. "I talked to the widow and she's never seen Kenny Burk before."

"Damn," Kelsey said, her voice barely above a whisper. "Well, we tried."

"Yeah." He started the engine and buckled his seatbelt, his heart lodged in his throat. *Please don't let anything happen to her. Please.* "Uh, hey," he said, trying to sound as casual as possible. "Think maybe you can come home early today? I can make us dinner and we can go over some case stuff again."

"I'll try," she said. "I've got to go. I'll text you when I leave."

"Okay." *I love you.* The words hovered on the tip of his tongue, but he bit them back. Now wasn't the time. Let him catch Phil and get Kelsey out of danger, and then he'd sort through his mess of feelings and his confusion over the future. He hooked up his phone to the Bluetooth in the car, then pulled away from the curb, asking his phone to call Neal as he drove back toward the city as fast as he dared.

"Ward Investigation," his brother said, picking up on the second ring.

"Hey, it's Ryan," he said, rounding a curve. "I need you to do something for me."

"Sure. What's up?"

"Go over to the US Marshals' field office where Kelsey works and get her out of there ASAP."

With Kelsey, he'd been careful to keep the urgency from creeping into his tone, but there was no hiding it from his family. They knew him too well. So, of course, Neal picked up on it right away.

"What's wrong?" his brother asked, tone terse.

"The guy we've been looking for? It's her boss. And she and an intern are alone in the office with him right now."

"Shit," Neal bit out. "You need to tell her to get out of there."

"I *can't*," Ryan growled out. "You don't understand—she's a *terrible* liar. The second she heard that Phil's our guy, she'd give the whole thing away, and God only knows what Phil would do in response. I can't tell her the truth while she's anywhere near him—and neither can you. Just…go over there and make up some excuse as to why she needs to leave right away."

"Will do. I'm on my way out the door right now."

"I'll owe you a thousand," Ryan said. "Thanks, bro."

He hung up, feeling a tad better that his brother would be there and Kelsey would be protected. Once she found out what was really going on, he was sure she'd be pissed as hell at him for keeping all this shit from her. But it really was the best option for her own protection and safety. Not to mention the integrity of their mission. She had to understand that. She just had to.

14

———

Kelsey had just finished typing up yet another case report when the front door opened. She looked up more out of habit than anything, then did a doubletake. Neal Ward? What the hell was he doing there?

Phil stood up from his desk near the door, scowling. "Can I help you, sir?"

"Uh, no." Neal locked eyes on Kelsey and made a beeline for her desk in the back. "I'm here to see her. Agent Poppins."

"What are you doing here?" Kelsey asked him when he arrived at her desk. "This isn't really a good time."

Neal glanced over his shoulder at Phil, who was still watching them like a hawk, then cleared his throat. "I found some information on that lead you asked about, Agent Poppins. I came to tell you in person because it's time-sensitive. Can we go outside?"

She frowned, trying to read his pointed look. She didn't know what was going on, but it seemed clear that it was urgent. Neal wasn't the type to make mountains out of molehills either, so at the clear distress she saw in his eyes, her pulse kicked higher. Whatever he was doing here, it had to be pretty bad for him to come in person. Kelsey swallowed hard and nodded. "Uh, yes. Fine. I'm due for a break anyway." She pulled her purse out of her desk drawer, then followed Neal to the entrance, saying to Phil in passing. "Be right back."

Her boss didn't respond, just watched them walk out, his expression grim.

"What the hell, Neal?" she asked, once they'd walked across the parking lot to the strip mall where vending machines lined one exterior wall of the structure. "Why are you here? What's happening?" Her stomach dropped as another thought occurred to her, worse than the others. "Oh God. Is Ryan okay?"

"Yes, he's fine." Neal looked from her to the Marshals' office across the way and then back again, still keeping his voice low. "Ryan called me and asked me to get you out of the office. We need to go—right away. He's heading straight to our dad's house, and he's promised that he'll explain everything once we get there. Here, let's take your car— I can pick mine up later."

They drove in relative silence, which only gave Kelsey more time to catastrophize in her own head. She knew Ryan had been continuing to follow up leads from the apartment building incident. Maybe he'd finally found something. That would be good, right? Except why would she need to leave her office for him to tell her? They usually shared whatever updates he'd been able to find over dinner each night. Sending his brother to come get her, without any explanation, felt awfully cloak and dagger. What could have caused it?

At the house, Neal let her in and tried to be a good host, offering her something to drink. But she didn't want a beverage—she wanted answers. Thankfully, she didn't have long to wait for them. They'd only been at the house for ten minutes or so when Ryan came screeching into the driveway. Kelsey stepped outside to meet him and

Ryan all but sprang out of the driver's seat to meet her. He immediately pulled Kelsey into a bear hug, holding her tight and whispering over and over into her hair, "I'm so glad you're okay."

Anxiety built inside her, heavy and hard, and she pulled free, hands shaking slightly. "What's going on, Ryan?"

"It's Phil," Ryan said bluntly, scraping a hand through his hair. "He's the murderer, not Kenny Burk. That's why I had to get you out of there before he tried to hurt you again, Kelsey. He was right fucking there the whole time."

"No. Wait a minute." She backed up a step, then another, mind racing. "It's not Phil. It can't be. He wasn't even in town when the Stephenson murder happened."

Ryan shook his head. "He didn't have to be here—he'd already ordered the murder, and probably paid the guy to do it. And then he killed that prison guard to cover his tracks."

Kelsey just blinked at him, numb, as she tried to fit those pieces together. Her boss wasn't her most favorite person in the world, but he wasn't a killer. Couldn't be. Right? She somehow managed to reach the sofa and flop down, her purse sliding down her arm to the floor with a dull thud. "I don't understand."

"I know this is a shock," Ryan said, sitting next to her and putting his arm around her shoulders to pull her into his side, his body warm against her. It did nothing to chase away the chill inside her, though. "But it's true. The prison guard's widow confirmed it. I showed her the picture you sent me, the one from the Christmas party, and she positively identified Phil as the man who'd come to talk to her husband on October fourteenth. You said he left town on the fifteenth for his trip, right? He must have taken care of this right before he left. I'm not sure if he was deliberately looking to set up an alibi for himself or if it was just chance, the prisoner transfer happening when he was already scheduled to be out of town, but now that we know what the connection really is, we've lost the one reason why we eliminated him as a suspect in the first place."

For a minute, Kelsey just absorbed the information, struggling to process it. She couldn't argue with Ryan's conclusion. Phil really was the guy. He was the one who had killed those prisoners, who had killed the prison guard, who had tried to kill her. And she'd been all but alone with him in the office just minutes ago. The very thought made her skin crawl. But…why had Ryan left her in that office without warning her? Yes, he'd sent Neal, but Neal hadn't arrived until a good ten minutes after she'd hung up with Ryan. Anything could have happened in those ten minutes. Why hadn't he warned her?

"Ryan, why didn't you tell me any of this on the phone?"

"Because," he started, then hesitated, wincing as he looked down at his feet. "Because I know you can't keep a secret, Kelsey, and I didn't want you to put yourself or the intern in danger if you knew."

Now it was Kelsey's turn to wince. She knew he had a point, but still. "I might not be able to lie, Ryan, but there were other things I could've done. I could've told you to call Phil and distract him while I got the intern and myself outside. You and I could have come up with another excuse to explain my reaction, the way we did when Phil caught us in the office the first time. Hell, I could've pulled the fire alarm and snuck away in the chaos. There were other options. Options that respected my right to know, and my ability to take reasonable action. Options that showed you trusted me."

It felt like their argument over his job all over again, with him keeping secrets and her feeling left out of the process, as if her insight didn't count and shouldn't be considered. But it was worse this time because it was her *job,* her *workplace* that was under threat, while he hadn't trusted her enough to let her in on what was going on. They could still fix this, though. With his job situation, he had apologized and admitted that he'd been in the wrong. If he did that now, if he made it clear that he *did* respect her and saw her as a capable partner—not a vulnerable target who needed to be coddled—then she could forgive him. They could move forward.

Just apologize, she willed him silently. *Say you're sorry. Say you're sorry. Say you're sorry.*

"I'm sorry—" he said, and some of the tension released from her shoulders. But then he continued, and the tension came back even stronger. "—that you're upset, but it seemed like the best option to protect you. Honestly, I'd make the same choice again. I'll always make the call that's best for the mission and the safety of everyone involved, even if it hurts your feelings."

And that was…just about the worst thing he could have said. First, there was never any woman in the history of ever who wanted an apology that started with "I'm sorry you're upset, but…" And beyond that, he still wasn't acknowledging the main issue here. With his actions, he'd made it clear that it was his choice, his decision that mattered. Not theirs. Not hers. So much for working together on this case. Or the future.

Not to mention, *he was wrong.* He was acting as if he took the only option that kept her safe, but she couldn't help thinking that he might have even put her in *more* danger with his choice. "How can you be so sure you made the right call? You chose the one that kept me in the dark about everything and left me even more vulnerable, because I still trusted Phil at that point when I shouldn't have."

"I sent Neal right over—" Ryan argued.

"And he arrived ten minutes later," she said. "In those ten minutes, what if Phil had asked me to go somewhere with him? I'd have gone without a second thought because I thought he was in the clear as a suspect. You wanted to do all the work to keep me safe, but I'm a trained, experienced law enforcement professional, Ryan. I don't need to be protected. I need to you to trust me to be able to protect *myself.*" She took a deep breath to ease the constriction in her chest. "Look, I get that we have different strengths we bring to the table, different training, and maybe that makes it harder for you to see us as full partners. But if you look at what happened today and still think you made the right call by keeping important information from me and by not seeing me as a full, capable partner in this case, then none of this is going to work between us."

He stopped pacing and just stared at her, so long she wondered if he'd frozen that way. Excruciating seconds ticked by in silence, until finally he said, "Are you talking professionally or personally?"

It killed her to say it, to stick to her guns, but she had to. She'd worked too hard to get where she was to throw it all away on a man who—like all the other men before him—couldn't accept and respect every side of her. She forced out her answer. "Both."

"Fuck." He turned away and slammed a fist against the wall, hard enough to knock the pictures there askew. His cheeks were red and his eyes angry. She wasn't scared of him turning that anger on her. Ryan wasn't that kind of person. But all the same, it told her what she needed to know. He wasn't going to apologize, wasn't going to back down. And that meant this was over.

"I know you want me to apologize," he said, his voice low and pained. "But I can't. I did what I thought was best and I stand by my decision." He squeezed his eyes shut and let his head fall back. "I knew this wouldn't work out. I'm no good at relationships, Kelsey, never have been, because the mission always came first. It still does."

"Uh," Neal said, sticking his head in and looking sheepish. "Sorry to interrupt, but you guys really need to go report all this to my contact at the police department ASAP. Especially if you're not one-hundred-percent sure the Internal Affairs Department is clean. The police are your best bet to get this guy put away.”

Ryan stared at her for a long moment, a muscle ticking in his cheek, then headed for the door. “Let’s go.”

Kelsey wanted to tell him where he could stick his orders, but dammit. Neal was correct.

“Yep.” She gave Neal a final look, the knot of sadness inside her pulling, then stood with as much grace as possible and slung her purse over her shoulder before following Ryan outside. He was back in business-mode, avoiding eye contact and not speaking to her at all. That was fine, really. She had nothing left to say because all this was just more proof. Proof that Ryan could never be the partner she needed. And while it felt like her world was ending, she’d be okay. She had to be. She’d get through it like she always did, on her own.

15

The drive to the police station was a slow-motion hell. At least that was what it felt like to Ryan. He couldn't wrap his head around Kelsey's reaction just now. How could she perceive his actions so differently from the way he'd intended them? Everything he'd done was to protect her. How was that a bad thing? He'd seen the danger to her, and he'd just reacted. It had worked, she'd gotten out safely. Wasn't that what mattered? Apparently not, since their relationship was now over.

He drove with one hand, the other elbow resting against the window ledge, hand rubbing his forehead. The tension inside him was building higher, like it was all coming to a head—the end of his military career, the loss of his father, the break-up with Kelsey. He needed to keep his shit together now or risk falling apart completely.

They reached the police station and walked in, still not looking or saying a word to each other. Ryan went up to the counter and asked to speak with Detective Simon, the cop who his brother had assured him they could trust. Instead of the brawny white guy Ryan had expected to walk out, a short curvy black woman walked up to him.

"You Ryan Ward?" she asked him, her gaze speculative.

"Yep." He forced a smile and shook her hand. "Detective Simon?"

"That's me." She turned next and introduced herself to Kelsey. "Come with me. Hear you guys are in quite a pickle."

"That's an understatement," Kelsey said.

They went to a quiet office in the back of the station and Detective Simon closed the door, giving them privacy. She took a seat behind her desk while Ryan and Kelsey sat in the chairs in front of it.

"So," the detective started. "Neal filled me in a little bit. Marshal Poppins, sounds like you got at least one dirty Marshal at your office?"

Kelsey nodded. "Yes. And please, call me Kelsey." She glanced at Ryan, then away fast. "We've gathered enough evidence to have good reason to believe that my boss, Commander Phil Johnson, is responsible for multiple murders of inmates over the past few years—and tried to kill us as well."

"I see." Detective Simon sat back in her chair, fingers steepled as she took that in. "Neal wasn't kidding when he said this was big. Have you contacted your Internal Affairs Department about this?"

"We have, but we're not sure they can be trusted. There's a possibility someone in IA is in on it," Ryan added and both women's gazes darted to him. He cleared his throat and frowned. "One attempt on our lives happened right after we went to them about our initial suspicions regarding Commander Johnson. That's why we came to you with this. Harder for him to cover his tracks with another law enforcement group involved."

"Right," Detective Simon said, sitting forward. "Walk me through what's happened so far." Thankfully, she already knew all the backstory about the case his dad had been working on, so they were able to pick up the story with the conversation at the shooting range and their agreement to work together. They laid it all out for her, starting with his initial suspicion, confirmed by the transport records, through their conversations with the receptionist and the prison guard, and then the conversation with the prison guard's widow. They also detailed the attacks they'd experienced.

"Well, I commend you both on all the work you've done so far on this. I'll take it from here. I'd recommend you both lie low for a while, until we get this resolved. Marshal Poppins," Simon held up a hand. "Sorry. Kelsey. I'd suggest you call in sick to work for a few days. And this probably goes without saying, but you should stay somewhere other than your usual residence, or any residence that might be included in your file as an emergency contact. Apprehending a marshal is a big deal and it will take us several days to get all the appropriate people and agencies on board for this. Plus, we'll need warrants issued. So, just hold tight until you hear from me again. Understood?"

They both nodded and stood.

Detective Simon came around the desk to walk them back out to the lobby. "It was nice meeting you both." She turned at the desk to give them both a meaningful look. "You know, you really are a great team. I hope you continue to work together in the future."

Damn. Wasn't that just like salt in the wound for Ryan? He hazarded a glance at Kelsey, but she was stoic as she shook the detective's hand again, then headed outside without him. Ryan jogged to catch up with her, painfully aware of exactly what he was losing by her walking away, but feeling powerless to stop it. Just like he'd been powerless to salvage his military career. Just like he'd been powerless to stop his dad from dying. The heavy weight of guilt and grief in his chest dropped lower into his gut.

After a deep breath, he climbed in behind the wheel of his car and started the engine. It felt like he needed to say something, but he wasn't sure what exactly. He ended up coming out with, "You can stay at my dad's place with me, if you want. There's plenty of room, since it's just me most of the time. Neal lives with Lori and Lance is in DC during the week and usually staying with Ruth when he's here for weekends. You can have your own room and—"

"I'd rather get a hotel room, thanks." Her words hung like icicles in the air. "I've moved people before in witness protection—I know how to stay under the radar."

"Phil knows all of that, too," Ryan said, knowing the reply would probably piss her off but feeling the need to bring it up anyway.

"Sure, but even if Phil did manage to get information about where I'm staying from the motel clerk—which is unlikely because he'd have to call every motel in the city *and* convince those people to talk to him—he's too smart to openly attack me." She shook her head. "There'd be no way for him to get to my room without leaving a trail of evidence." She crossed her arms and pressed herself against the door, as if trying to get as far away from Ryan as possible. His heart broke a little more. "I'll be fine on my own. I'll be cautious and stay in my room until they arrest Phil. Just take me back to your place so I can pick up my car, and I'll take it from there."

"Kelsey, please." He raked a hand through his hair, that burgeoning tension inside him making him more agitated by the second. "This isn't—"

She held up a hand, palm out toward him. "I need space, Ryan. From you, from the case, from everything. Just get me to my car and I'll call you later with the address and room information, okay?"

No. It most definitely wasn't okay with him, but he did what she asked, watching Kelsey drive off into the gathering gloom, feeling like his entire world had gone to shit. He wanted to go after her, beg her to stay, but deep down he knew that wouldn't solve anything. So he went inside his dad's empty house.

He thought he'd feel better there, surrounded by the past, surrounded by all the things that were familiar, that were home, but he didn't. Maybe because Lance had already worked so hard to clear out a lot of stuff. The place felt empty now, a shell of what he remembered growing up. It didn't help that he was alone, either. It was way too quiet here. Way too lonely, too.

Ryan ate a bologna sandwich that he didn't even taste, then grabbed a beer and decided to go to bed early. It had been a shitty day. Best to put it behind him and start fresh tomorrow. Except once he was lying there, staring up at the ceiling, all he could think about was Kelsey. The flowery scent of her shampoo, the brightness of her smile, the sound of her laughter, the feel of her in his arms, so warm and soft and perfect.

Fuck.

His eyes began to sting and burn and no matter how hard he blinked, it didn't go away. He rubbed them too, but it didn't help. Shit. Now they were watering like crazy and his nose was running and…

Dammit.

He was crying. And once he'd started he couldn't seem to stop. All of it poured over him, drowning him in sorrow—grief over losing Kelsey, grief over losing his dad, this big old empty house where he'd laughed and cried and had his first kiss and his first break-up and all the memories of his childhood that would be sold to the highest bidder in the very near future. Gone. It was all gone.

His career, his future, everything he cared for gone.

Ryan buried his face in the pillow and had a good, long sob-fest. When he was done, empty and aching inside, he rolled onto his back and stared at the ceiling again, nose stuffed up and eyes swollen. With all that out of his system, his brain kicked into high gear again, showing him a montage of all the things he didn't want to happen in his life. He didn't want to end up like his dad did, bitter and broken-hearted for half of his life, unable to move on after losing the woman he loved.

Kelsey.

Man, he missed her so much it hurt. He loved her. And he'd lost her. Mainly because of his own stupidity. He'd gotten tunnel vision on the mission, paying attention only to the end result that he wanted without realizing how much he was screwing up.

Shit, shit, shit. He sat up and scrubbed a hand over his hair and face. Grabbed a tissue and blew his nose, then picked up his phone. His SEAL training was still deeply ingrained, telling him that the last thing you wanted to do on a mission was give up. Even when things looked darkest, you came up with a plan, executed it, saw things through to the other side. It was what had gotten him in trouble there at the end, but his instincts said it might be what would save him now, even if he had no clue what his next step should be.

Still, he might know someone who could guide him. Ryan hit the speed dial button for Neal and waited for his brother to pick up.

"What's going on?" Neal said once he answered. "Did you talk to Detective Simon?"

"Yeah. It's in her hands now." Ryan sighed and hung his head. "I lied."

"To the police?" Neal sounded confused.

"No, bro. To you." He cursed under his breath, then came out with it, difficult as it was. "When I told you about leaving the military, I said that it was for the best—that I was okay with it. I lied. I'm not okay with it. Not at all. And I messed up earlier, when I told you to go get Kelsey at her office instead of just telling her what was going on myself. She doesn't want anything to do with me now and I don't blame her. I'm a fucking mess. Just like Dad. And I'm not okay with him being alone at the end of his life, either. Jesus. What if I end up like that? All alone and bitter as fuck and unable to let people in…"

He had to stop because his chest squeezed so tight he couldn't breathe. He was spiraling again.

Neal exhaled slowly. "Shit. Calm down, Ry. It's okay. You're okay. Things aren't that bad. There's a way out and we're going to find it, okay?"

Ryan nodded, even though his brother couldn't see, not trusting his voice.

"And as far as Dad being lonely at the end of his life," Neal continued, "I'm not sure that's true. It's not how Lori describes him, anyway. She says he had tons of friends and colleagues he cared about. And maybe he wasn't dating anyone romantically, but he'd still reconnected with you and Lance and Ruth." Neal chuckled. "To hear Lori talk about it, his biggest regret was that he started working on all of those relationships so late. He spent too long throwing himself into work. If he'd just taken the time he needed, grieved my mom, and moved on, he could have been happier in the long run."

A beat or two passed as Ryan took that in, new questions forming. "Is that what I'm doing? Focusing all my attention on this case so I don't have to deal with things outside of it?"

"Maybe," Neal said, always a straight-shooter. "I don't know, Ry. Only you have the answer to that. I know it's easier, going from mission to mission rather than figuring out a bigger life plan—but that doesn't mean it's better. The one thing I do know is that Dad would be so proud of you for saving all those hostages. And for trying so hard to weed out the corruption at the Marshals' office and to keep Kelsey safe. Hell, we're all proud of you, little bro. Don't ever forget that, okay?"

Ryan got all choked up again, for completely different reasons now. He wasn't sure what he'd do without his family. They were the most important thing to him. Well, besides Kelsey. But honestly, she felt like family now too. She was a part of him. A part he never wanted to lose. He just had to figure out how to make up for his awful mistakes.

"Thanks, bro," he said. "Talk to you in the morning."

"Night," Neal said, ending the call.

He lay back down again, not ready to sleep, but not quite so worked up now either. He closed his eyes and thought about how to make it up to Kelsey, eventually drifting off to pictures of her smiling in his head.

16

The next morning, Ryan woke up feeling surprisingly refreshed. He'd actually slept better than he'd expected the night before, probably because he'd exhausted himself emotionally. He got dressed and got ready for the day, then went downstairs to make coffee. He was almost to the kitchen when his phone buzzed in his jeans pocket and he pulled it out to answer without checking the caller ID. Neal, most likely, checking up on him to make sure he was okay.

"Ryan here," he said, flipping on the kitchen lights and squinting until his eyes adjusted.

"Hello, Mr. Ward."

The male voice on the other end of the line froze him in his tracks. He knew that voice from Kelsey's office, interrupting him and Kelsey in their first kiss. Phil Johnson.

Adrenaline flooded his system and his throat dried. Wide awake now, he gripped the doorframe, pulse galloping faster than a thoroughbred. Kelsey. All he could think about was Kelsey.

"What do you want, Johnson?" he croaked out past his tight vocal cords.

Phil chuckled. "Very good, Ward. Glad you remember me."

"I never forget a lying asshole." Ryan's chest tightened. "How did you get this number?"

"Well, it's a funny thing." Something creaked through the phone line behind Phil. A chair, maybe. "You see, we keep logs of all calls going through the Marshals' office phone lines, Ward. And I happened to see this number appear on Kelsey's call list yesterday. I've been monitoring her line, you see, since that time I caught you two behaving inappropriately in the office. Can't have that sort of behavior in here."

"Right." Ryan gritted his teeth. "God forbid we behave *inappropriately.* But murdering people is fine, huh?"

"Murder is such a harsh word, Mr. Ward." Phil's tone turned chiding. "They were criminals. Scum. Is the world really worse off without them in it? I think not. Society doesn't have to pay to house and feed them, the families of the victims get a sense of closure, and I get a considerably healthier bank account just for taking out the trash. It's a win all around, don't you think? Maybe I skirted some rules, but it was all for the greater good. That's an explanation you can understand, isn't it? I've seen your military records, Ryan. I'm sure you know what I'm talking about."

Ice shivered down his spine. "How the fuck—"

"I've got contacts everywhere, Ryan. People who owe me favors. When I call them in, people comply."

Phil had just gone from a mid-level asshole on Ryan's shit list straight to the top spot. "What do you want?" he repeated, voice low and lethal.

"Were the frayed brake lines not clear enough? How about the scene in the studio apartment? Surely you've realized what I want—you and Kelsey out of my way."

"I swear to God, if you hurt one hair on Kelsey's head I will take you out personally."

"Aw, how sweet." Phil gave a derisive snort. "But at the moment Marshal Poppins is much more valuable to me whole, hairs and all. Until that changes. I'm actually watching her right now, through the window in her room at the Lazy Eight Motel."

Oh fuck. Fuck, fuck, fuck. A crater opened inside him, dark and full of despair. Because Phil was right—that was Kelsey's current location. Ryan had the text message to prove it. But how the hell had Phil figured it out?

Ryan's SEAL training kicked into high gear, running through scenarios and strategies at breakneck speed. Phil could be bluffing about knowing where Kelsey was, but Ryan couldn't take that chance until he knew for certain.

"Lazy Eight?" he said, playing it off, trying to suss out more information from his opponent. "Now I know you're lying. That place is a dump. Kelsey wouldn't set foot in there in a billion years."

"Oh, Ryan." Phil laughed, cold and harsh. "I've been doing this job almost as long as you've been alive. Don't treat me like an amateur. It's Marshal 101. Standard operating procedure. Check into some anonymous hotel in the area and lie low." He sighed. "Now obviously, I couldn't call every one of them in Detroit. Talk about amateur hour. No. I just put in a report that we had a rogue marshal and for any motel with information about her whereabouts to contact me. Well, guess what? One of them did."

Shit. Yep. Phil was good. Since they hadn't been able to arrest him immediately, he still had access to all his resources as a marshal. And he'd put them to work. But he still might be bluffing about having eyes on Kelsey, and about being willing to attack. He remembered what Kelsey had said about Phil not taking the chance, knowing it would leave too much evidence behind. And he had faith in her knowledge and experience as a marshal—enough to question whether she'd let herself be visible by leaving her room or standing by a window. He trusted Kelsey. And he sure as hell didn't trust Phil. So he was going to verify. "What's she wearing?"

"Excuse me?"

"Kelsey. What's she wearing? If you're looking at her right now like you say you are, tell me what she's wearing."

Phil exhaled slowly, then rattled off an outfit, same as what Kelsey had been wearing the day before. "I really don't have time for this, Mr. Ward. In fact, maybe I'll just kill her now and be done with it."

"No!" Ryan's voice echoed through the quiet kitchen. Whether Phil was bullshitting him or not, the idea of Kelsey being killed was one he couldn't risk. "What do you want from me?"

"Now, there's a good question, Ryan. See, I knew you could do it if you thought hard enough."

Yep. As soon as he got his hands on this guy, it was gonna hurt. Bad. Still, he swallowed down his anger and focused on Kelsey's safety.

"I want you to meet me," Phil continued. "At the abandoned high school near you in…" A beat passed. "Let's say twenty minutes. Come alone and don't even think about bringing backup or warning Kelsey. I've got eyes and ears on her at all times and I'll know. You and I both know she can't lie for shit. So even if you do manage to get through to her somehow, I'll see it on her face. And I will kill her. Understand?"

If it were possible to reach through the phone line and strangle Phil with his bare hands, Ryan would have done it in a heartbeat. As it was, he had little choice but to agree. "I'll be there."

Phil ended the call and Ryan stood in the empty, quiet kitchen, feeling like he'd just been struck by a Mack truck. It took him a moment to get his bearings again, chaos firing in his brain, bouncing between Kelsey and Phil and the danger she was in.

He sank down in the kitchen chair and dropped his head into his hands. *Okay. Think. Think.*

There had to be a way out of this. A solution. He just had to come up with it. Part of him wanted to do what Phil asked, no questions, because he couldn't risk Kelsey's life. Plus, he didn't have much time for strategizing. The old high school building was about fifteen minutes away from his dad's house. In five minutes or less, he needed to be out the door. Not exactly ideal.

And yet when he stopped to think past the initial panic, he was reminded that something felt off, fishy. Kelsey was too capable to leave herself exposed. Phil had tried to make sure Ryan wouldn't contact Kelsey, had said that it would only harm her, but who was he going to believe? Kelsey, who said she knew what she was doing? Or Phil, who had implied that she was mistaken? Fuck that—of course he trusted Kelsey.

And that meant his best option was to reach out to her, bring her into the loop and let her be part of the plan. Instead of calling, though, he thumbed in a quick text, hoping she'd get it in time. *"Keep your head down and walk calmly to the bathroom NOW. Text me when you're there."*

The next few seconds ticked by like a small eternity. Those three little dots on his screen jumping in time with his racing heart. Just when he was walking out the door to his car, her reply came through.

"Done."

As he climbed into his car and started the engine to let it warm up, he typed in a brief explanation about what was happening. *"Phil called. Knows your location. Claims he has eyes and ears on you and will shoot to kill unless I meet him in 15 min at the old high school. On my way. Described you wearing outfit from yesterday."*

More dots as he put the phone on Bluetooth in the car and pulled out of the driveway. He got about a half a block before another ding sounded.

"His intel is old. Def. no eyes on me." More dots, then, *"No ears either. Swept room for bugs last night. None—haven't left it since. Window nearly touching brick wall of building next door. Wearing different outfit today."*

Relief washed over him, sweet and swift, before his adrenaline kicked in again. He used the voice to text feature on his phone to reply as he drove to the high school. *"Still going to meet Phil. But plan to take him down when I get there. Worst case, I keep him occupied while you call my brothers to come help."*

"No! Phil is more dangerous than you think. And he's desperate. If he gets lucky and escapes or kills you, then we have no way of catching him again." More dots. *"Better plan. Go in with a recording device and try to get a confession. Keep him distracted until we get there. Do it clean. Less risky. Then we all take him down."*

Dammit. The cave man part of Ryan didn't want to be smart and strategic and draw out a confession—he just wanted to pound the living daylights out of the asshole who'd tried to kill Kelsey. All the same, he knew a good plan when he saw one. He could use his phone to record Phil, if he could figure out the app. He turned into the deserted high school parking lot and cut the engine. No immediate sign of Phil, but he had to be there. Ryan was already a couple minutes late because of the traffic lights. *"Fine. We do it your way. Nearly there. Call my brothers. Send backup. I'm going in."*

17

Ryan checked his service weapon and got out of the car, slowly approaching the front door, checking his surroundings for a set-up. He'd set his phone to record and put it in his jacket pocket, so that was ready to go, per his plan with Kelsey. Now, he just had to find Phil and get him talking while he waited for the others to show up.

He reached the front doors and slipped inside, thinking he'd find a spot that gave him a tactical advantage over his opponent if things went south. Ryan barely made it two steps before there was a loud bang and pain exploded through his left thigh.

Teeth gritted, he fell to the floor, his weapon clattering away as he gripped his leg, already gushing blood.

"You're late," Phil said, stepping out of the shadows, gun still pointed at Ryan.

"You shot me!" Ryan said. Stating the obvious, sure, but then he'd been fucking shot, so… "What the hell?"

Unfortunately, being injured also changed up the trajectory of their strategy here. As he struggled to breathe and assess how badly he was hurt, Ryan's mind continued to run through the facts, his SEAL training locked in. Okay. He was way more vulnerable now, regardless of where the bullet had struck him. If he was going to attack Phil, he'd need to do it *now*. If he waited and tried to get his confession, he'd just get weaker as he lost more and more blood. While he was reasonably sure he could still win a fight right now, he couldn't swear he'd be able to in ten minutes. And it would probably be in ten minutes or so that Kelsey and his brothers would get there, walking into a situation where Ryan would be almost useless to protect her.

But what was it Kelsey had said the previous day? *I don't need to be protected. I need to you to trust me to be able to protect* myself.

He did trust her, with everything he had. And he was going to stick to her plan. The phone in his pocket dug into his hip beneath him and he said a silent prayer that the thing was still recording. He just had to get Phil to talk. Shouldn't be hard since the guy was such an arrogant asshole. Ryan just had to keep his wits about him and wait for the cavalry that he knew was on its way. He didn't have to save the day on his own this time. He just had to hold it together until they arrived…and try not to bleed out before then.

Shit. It hurt so bad.

Stay calm. Stay focused. Stay on mission.

Right. Okay. He could do this. Had been trained to do this. Ryan swallowed hard and looked up at Phil again, to find the guy watching him with a raised brow, expression impassive, like he was picking out produce at the supermarket instead of contemplating homicide. His gun was still pointed at Ryan, finger on the trigger. Such a dick.

He could use that though, Phil's ego, against him. Phil thought he had control of the situation. What would he do if Ryan hinted otherwise?

How would that unravel him? With few other options at the moment and needing to stall until the others arrived, that was what he did. "Kind of sloppy, don't you think?" he hissed as he tried to move, slipping on his own blood on the slick floor. "If you kill me now, how will you know who else Kelsey and I told about you and what you did?"

Phil scowled. "You're going to tell me. You're going to spill anything I want to know," he said as he pulled a set of handcuffs out of his pocket.

Ryan tsked, giving Phil his best shit-eating grin. If there was one thing Ryan Ward knew how to do, it was be an aggravating dick. And to guys like Phil, who expected everything to be just so, who were used to being in charge and having others snap to do whatever they said, nothing could be as unsettling as someone who refused to show them any iota of respect.

Asshole Ryan: Take One. Lights, camera, action!

"It's adorable, really," Ryan said, "you thinking you've got this all locked down. Don't you realize what a mess you've made of the whole thing, Philly boy? All the clues you left? Amateur hour, from start to finish."

"That's not true," Phil spat out through gritted teeth. "I'm in control. *I'm* in control of all of it. With one word, I could have Kelsey—"

Ryan scoffed. "With one word, you couldn't do shit to Kelsey. Did you really think I bought your stupid bluff?" He made a loud buzzer noise. "Sorry, try again! Go on, Phil. Impress me. Tell me how this is all part of your bullshit plan."

"Oh, I'll tell you, all right," Phil said, roughly fastening the cuff around Ryan's wrist. "We're going to go into a classroom and I'll tell you *exactly* why you should be afraid of me—and then you're going to tell me *everything* you've found out and who knows about it."

Ryan faked a yawn. "Sorry, were you saying something? I started tuning out when you went all 'blah, blah, I'm in control, blah, blah, bow before me, blah, blah, I'm scary and intimidating.' He looked Phil over critically. "I feel like the paunch kind of undercuts the intimidation factor. Too long at a desk job, right? Do you want me to recommend a good gym?"

Phil went absolutely red with rage, grabbing Ryan's other wrist and cuffing it too, before dragging Ryan down the hall. He was so caught up in his anger that he didn't even notice Ryan laying down the St. Jude medallion—the one the hostage had given him. Hopefully Kelsey would remember their conversation in the car and know something was up, that things weren't going to plan.

She was on her way, he knew that without a shadow of a doubt. He just had to hold on until then.

Kelsey raced toward the high school with Neal, Lance, and Lori all on speakerphone with her. She had a bad feeling about all this, and a burning fear that they would be too late. While she trusted Ryan to do the right thing, she didn't trust her asshole boss Phil at all. She was, in fact, pretty disgusted with herself that she'd ever trusted him. She wasn't sure what pissed her off more about the whole situation—the fact he'd lied to all of them for so many years about his corruption, or the fact that she'd believed him.

She liked to think of herself as a good judge of character, but she'd completely misread Phil Johnson. Yes, she'd never really warmed up to the man, but it had never even occurred to her that he could be dirty.

God, maybe Ryan was right. Maybe she did have blind spots. Maybe they did work better as a team than separately. Even if things were rocky sometimes.

"I'm calling the police now," Lori said, jarring Kelsey out of her heartache and back to business.

"Okay," Kelsey said. "Thanks. Neal and Lance, what's your ETA?"

"On our way now," Lance said. "We'll meet you at the school. Wait for us there and we'll figure out a plan of attack together."

"See you soon." She ended the call, and sped into the parking lot a few minutes later. The first thing she saw was Ryan's car parked near the old front entrance, alone. That bad feeling in her gut turned into a crater of foreboding.

After checking her service weapon, Kelsey got out of her car and headed for the front entrance, her Glock low and at the ready, just in case. Outside the dusty glass doors at the front of the high school, Kelsey stopped in the corner, using the brick at her back as a shield in case Phil lurked just inside, and peered through the glass. Through the shadows, it was hard to see much, but there appeared to be a dark, dirty splotch on the floor. Not old and grubby like the rest, but fresh, wet even.

Shit. Taking a deep breath, she tried the door handles, found one that was open and slipped inside. Crouching slightly and sticking to the shadows to keep hidden as much as possible, Kelsey waited a moment, listening. Nothing. Slowly, she inched nearer the wet spot on the floor, keeping her weapon ready and surveying the area around her for threats.

As she reached it, several things hit her at once. First, the coppery smell in the air. Blood. Second, those streaks on the floor were fresh, confirming her suspicions. Someone had been hurt here recently. Heart in her throat and face flushed, she crouched again, spotting something in one pool of blood near her feet, the edge of it twinkling in the light from above.

Fingers shaking, she pulled it out and saw that it was a medallion. Not just any medallion. Ryan's St. Jude medallion, the one the hostage had given him after their rescue, which meant…

Oh God.

Ryan had to be the one hurt. Badly, given the amount of blood on the floor. Her stomach cramped and she thought she might vomit, not from nausea, but from pure fear. She loved him so much, and now she might lose him before she'd ever really had him. All because of Phil.

The anger inside her churned hotter, sending streaks of outrage through her limbs, and incinerating old cautions. Ryan had agreed to do things her way earlier and that had gotten him into this mess. Now, she was going to go rogue. Just like Ryan. Just for Ryan.

Kelsey had told Neal and Lance she'd meet them outside, that they'd go in together to take Phil down, but she couldn't wait. Not anymore. The man she loved was in danger, could be dying, and there was no way in hell she was going to sit around and wait for backup while that happened.

Jaw set tight, she straightened and continued down the hall. Her skin prickled with awareness as the light faded the further she got from the glass doors, and the shadows grew. Every step felt like a million, but she couldn't stop, wouldn't stop, following the streaks of Ryan's blood on the floor. She rounded a corner and started down yet another hall, gaze narrowed in the gathering gloom, when she heard it. A loud smacking sound, flesh on flesh.

Breath held, she neared a door near the end of the corridor and pressed her back to the cold metal locker on the wall behind her. This door had a rectangular glass panel in it, the lower right corner broken out. Through that small space, she heard Phil's voice and her grip tightened on her gun. Part of her wanted to find a clean shot and blow asshole Phil's head right off his body, but her training made her stop. She hadn't fully assessed the situation yet, and with Ryan's life in the balance, she could never take that chance. She might be doing this his way, but there was still some Kelsey left too.

"Tell me what the fuck you know. Right. Now!" More slaps, followed by pained grunts and the sound of someone spitting on the floor.

"Fuck you, asshole," Ryan said a moment later, and Kelsey grinned despite the situation. She'd never loved him more in her life. "I'm not telling you shit."

Phil gave an enraged growl and kicked something across the room, sending it clattering against the far wall. Kelsey was concerned it was Ryan, so she hazarded a quick glance through the glass panel in the door and found her Ryan cuffed to a chair in the middle of what had once been a classroom. All the old desks had been pushed to the perimeter and, based on where Phil was standing over a demolished one, that's what he'd kicked into the wall. She also noted the weapon in his hand before transferring her attention back to Ryan. Blood soaked the jeans over his right thigh and a thin red line trickled from the left corner of his mouth where Phil had struck him. But he was alive, for now.

Alive and pissed, if his belligerent expression was any indication.

Kelsey would take that over the alternative any day.

18

Ryan licked his lips, tasting salt and metal, then glared at Phil again. As far as he knew, his phone was still recording in his pocket and his captor was so rattled, he hadn't even checked for it. That was good.

What was bad was the fact that he'd lost a lot of blood. And it was getting harder and harder to focus. He blinked hard, his eyes gritty and stinging. *Think, dude. Think.* Keep him talking. Get him to confess.

"So," he said, wincing as his split lip pulled open once more and began to ooze again. "Gonna tell me your whole sob story? Mommy didn't hug you enough? Daddy thought you were dumb as shit? But you were going to prove them all wrong, weren't you? You were going to be a big success—a big shot, someone everyone would have to respect, right?" The signs were written all over him. Classic case of inferiority complex—a sad little bastard with a chip on his shoulder who thought he'd go out into the world and show them all why he was superior to them. It was never pretty when those guys figured out how mediocre they actually were.

Phil grumbled something Ryan didn't catch under his breath. The guy was still standing near the wall, staring down at the desk he'd kicked the shit out of after Ryan had told him to fuck off. For a second, he thought maybe the asshole hadn't heard him, but then he turned slowly, a flat look on his face that didn't bode well at all for Ryan's well-being.

"What would you know about it?" Phil asked, his tone deathly quiet, his face twisted in a sneer. "You jock types—everything comes so easily to you, doesn't it? Never any respect for those of us who have to work for it. All you have to do is bat your eyes and you get everything you want, don't you? Well, why shouldn't I get something? Years of working my ass off for the US Marshals and my salary is shit, nowhere near what I deserve. With Russo, I finally started getting what I should have had all along."

"By being errand boy for the mob? That's your big achievement?"

"I wasn't the errand boy!" Phil said, bristling. "Russo came to me and *I* was the one who figured it out. You think it was easy, working out how to drug those prisoners without anyone catching on? My own fucking partner never even had a clue! All I had to do was slip a little whiskey in his coffee—with a little wink and a nudge while I told him that it would keep him warm—and his alcoholism did the rest. He kept a flask in his pocket—it only took a taste to get him going. Half the time, he got so plastered, I could have led a line of can-can dancers through the transport van and he wouldn't have noticed."

Well, that answered one question: Kenny Burk was innocent. But was anyone else involved?

"Bullshit," Ryan taunted. "No way a desk case like you could handle injecting those prisoners all on your own. Who helped you? Was it the prison guards?"

"It was *me, I* did it!" Phil yelled, utterly infuriated. "I didn't need anyone's help—I did it all on my own. I took down every one of those fuckers." And there they had it—the confession. Or at least part of it.

"Pfft, no, you didn't. I know about Stephenson. Let the ball drop on that one, didn't you? And then you had to bring in someone else to take care of business."

"And I took care of that afterward, didn't I? No one even suspected that I was behind Patrick's death."

"But *I* sure as hell suspected something when I found that vodka bottle in Kelsey's car, didn't I? Getting lazy, Phil, pulling out the same trick twice. Did you really think it would work?" Ryan forced a chuckle, as if the thought of Kelsey in danger did anything other than fill him with rage.

Phil scowled. "You think that's funny? That this is a joke?"

Ryan sobered, but not before Phil was on him again, leaning his weight on his hands on either arm of the chair Ryan was strapped to. Asshole Phil leaned in nose to nose with him and sneered. "That will be the last thing you ever laugh at, you piece of shit." He grabbed Ryan's right thigh and squeezed hard, the fucker.

Ryan screamed, couldn't help it, doing his best to breathe and stay awake when all he wanted to do was pass out. As Ryan scrambled to get away, Phil released his thigh, his hand smacking against the phone in Ryan's pocket.

They both froze. Phil's gaze darted from Ryan's face to his jacket pocket and back again. But there was nothing Ryan could do to stop him when he reached into his pocket and pulled out the phone.

Shaken and sweaty, tears running down his cheeks, Ryan grinned. "Say hi to all those listeners at home, motherfucker!"

"You think I'm going down that easy?" Phil threw the phone on the floor and raised a foot to stomp on it.

"I wouldn't do that, if I were you. Destroying evidence is against the law," Kelsey said as the door crashed against the wall, her weapon drawn and aimed at Phil. "You've got enough on your rap sheet already, boss."

The way she said *boss* made it sound like the dirtiest curse word imaginable, and Ryan had never loved her more than at that moment. Then Phil drew his weapon and began shooting at her and Ryan's heart plummeted to his toes.

"Kelsey, no!" he screamed as she dived behind a stack of old desks. But before he could say anything more, Neal and Lance ran in and tried to tackle Phil. The asshole was too wily for them, though, and managed to get himself barricaded behind another stack of desks in the corner, firing at anything that moved. From where Ryan was, he could see Phil behind his barricade, firing at all the people Ryan loved most in the world, paying no attention at all to Ryan now.

Use that.

SEAL instincts still surging, Ryan summoned every last bit of strength he had to roll himself onto his side, then up onto his knees and finally his feet. Bullets were still flying, but he didn't care. Not anymore. If he could take Phil out, he could save everyone, and that was the most important thing. His right leg was completely numb, though somehow he managed not to topple over. He was cuffed to the chair, so he carried it with him, traversing the back of the classroom until he was behind Phil, a few feet away.

Pulse pounding and throat tight, memories of that ill-fated raid poured back into his head. Fighting against the odds, saving lives despite the personal risk. He'd do it all again a million times over if all those people were safe at the end of it. Would do it again now, to save those he loved.

Just then, Kelsey looked between a couple of the desks she was hiding behind and saw him, her face white and eyes huge.

He winked at her, then hefted the chair up and let it swing, smacking Phil hard on the back of the head with the chair legs. The blow knocked Phil into the wall. The double impact knocked him unconscious and he dropped to the floor.

Good thing, too, since the dizziness went haywire then and Ryan found himself staring up at the ceiling again as Kelsey rushed to his side and Neal and Lance went to restrain Phil.

"Ryan!" Kelsey cried, tears running down her face now, dripping onto Ryan's shirt. "Jesus. I thought he was going to kill you!"

"Same," he managed to croak out before his eyes closed and refused to open again. He felt Kelsey step away from him for a second, but she must have gone to get the handcuff key from Phil because when she came back, he felt her releasing his hands. That felt better—even if the rest of him was still in lousy shape. His leg was bad. He'd seen enough injuries to know. Something strong and tight wrapped around his upper right thigh and he managed to crack his eyes open enough to see it was Kelsey, using her belt as a tourniquet. Good girl. The best girl, really. He gave her a weak, wobbly smile. "You okay?"

"Ryan Ward. I can't believe you stuck to our plan to provoke him into a confession *when you'd been shot*!" She took a deep breath and shook her head. "I swear to God you took ten years off my life with that stunt. All that blood, knowing Phil had you trapped in here? And now you want to know if *I'm* okay? Hell no, I'm not okay!"

"Calm down," he said, feeling woozy again, gripping her hand to stay grounded. Ryan closed his eyes again and swallowed hard. "I trusted you. Knew you'd come. Knew you and my brothers could handle Phil as long as I did my part."

"You idiot," Kelsey said, then leaned down and kissed him, and that was when Ryan knew it would be okay. Maybe not the way he'd planned or wanted, but all right just the same. As long as Kelsey was kissing him, everything was fine. At the same moment, two other ideas occurred. One, that this team right here—him, Kelsey, his brothers, Lori who was undoubtedly playing her own role back at the office—was the best team he'd ever worked with. Even his SEAL team didn't compare, and that was saying something. And second, he owed Kelsey an apology.

He waited until she'd pulled back enough to let him speak, then said, "Hey. I'm sorry."

Kelsey cupped his cheeks and frowned down at him. "Ryan, I—"

"No," he insisted, coughing, then regretting it as more pain issued from his aching back muscles. Somewhere outside, sirens echoed from the parking lot and he knew it was now or never. "I need to get this out. All this time I was focused on all the ways my SEAL training made me different from you, instead of all the things we have in common and how well we fit together." His voice cracked and damn. He was thirsty. Thirstier than he ever remembered being in his life. But he forced himself to continue, his words rough. "We fit, Kelsey. In a crisis or out. You were right. I should have told you about Phil as soon as I found out. Maybe if I'd trusted you and your skills sooner, I wouldn't be here now, shot."

"Oh, Ryan." Kelsey bent again and kissed him, slow and sweet.

When she pulled back, he whispered, "I'm never making that mistake again."

Then more people were there and cops swarmed the area and EMTs came and loaded him onto a gurney. Whatever else Ryan had to say

would need to wait until later. He gave in to blissful unconsciousness
at last.

19

———————

Kelsey's frustration grew the longer she was stuck at the police station giving her statement. All she wanted was to be at the hospital, at Ryan's side. She loved him so much it hurt. She was glad that he'd apologized, but that wasn't even the point anymore. She didn't care about the mistakes that both of them had made in the past. Not when he'd proven her fears wrong, showing her that he truly respected and accepted her for who she was.

People said all sort of things. Look at Phil, who'd been lying to all of them for years. But today, Ryan had proved through his actions, beyond a shadow of a doubt, that he trusted her when it mattered most. Even when their plans went horribly wrong, he had her back. Always. Forever.

Her phone buzzed in her hand and she looked down from her seat in the busy station hallway to see another update from Lori. Bless her heart, she was by Ryan's side when Kelsey couldn't be. Kelsey was so grateful for that and for the constant updates on the man she loved. This said that Ryan was holding his own. They'd given him a couple of transfusions due to the amount of blood he'd lost, and then they'd taken him to surgery to remove the bullet from his right thigh and repair the internal damage it had caused. She knew he was under supervision and receiving the best care in the city, but still. The thought of Ryan lying there hurt in a hospital bed, while she was anywhere other than right by his side, broke her heart. She swallowed hard, blinking away the sudden sting of tears as she texted Lori back to thank her, then put her phone in her pocket.

God. She'd wasted so much time, so many years, so worried about whether a guy could accept her, want all of her, that she never stopped to ask if she accepted and wanted all of him. But with Ryan, there was no question. She wanted him. All of him. The good, the bad, and everything in between.

Which also meant that if he chose to take that paramilitary kidnapper-rescue-unit job, then she'd have to find a way to be okay with that because it was his decision. She realized now that if he was willing to try, so was she.

Does he want to try?

She sat back and stared down at her toes, waiting to be told she could finally leave. Honestly, Kelsey did think Ryan might want a relation-ship too, especially after that last kiss at the high school. There'd been plenty of adrenaline pumping through both their systems, yes. And they'd just survived a traumatic event, but that didn't make their feel-ings any less valid, right? And she'd sensed something in Ryan then —a peace, an understanding, a determination to…

"Ma'am," a uniformed officer said, then cleared his throat. "Sorry. Marshal Poppins. You are free to go now. If we have any additional questions, we'll call you."

"Thank you!" Kelsey was on her feet and halfway down the hall before he'd even finished speaking. Her phone buzzed in her pocket again, but she didn't bother to check it until she was in her car and ready to pull out of the lot. She'd expected to see another message from Lori. But instead, a message flashed up from the US Marshals' district office. She froze, blinking down at the screen in the twilight gloom inside the car. Fingers shaking slightly, she put the car back into park, then slid to open the full message. Read it once, then once again, to make sure she wasn't just imagining it all.

Nope.

The regional commander was asking her to step into Phil's old position, District Commander for Metro Detroit, as an interim appointment until they could formally find a replacement.

Oh God.

An odd mix of excitement and hesitation filled her. She'd always dreamed of a promotion like this, but it was coming at an awful time. She and Ryan had been through so much already and they still had so much to get through before they were done. Could they work through this too?

Right. Time to talk to Ryan and figure it out.

She dialed Lori's number and waited for it to connect. When Lori answered, Kelsey cut her off. "I'm sorry, I don't have a lot of time. I just got a message from regional that they want me to take over as interim commander at the field office until they find a replacement for Phil. I have to stop by there now and let everyone know what's going on before I can make it to the hospital and—"

"Hang on," Lori said, then the sounds of fumbling echoed through the line. When the next voice came on, it was the last one Kelsey expected to hear, but absolutely the one in the world she *wanted* to hear.

"Kelsey, honey?" Ryan said. His voice was rough and a bit groggy from the meds and anesthesia that was still wearing off, but just the sound of it flooded her with warmth all the same. "Listen, sweetheart. You go do what you need to do, okay? I'm so proud of you and I love you. Don't worry about me here. I'm fine. The docs said everything went well and I should make a full recovery. I'll see you when you're done, all right?"

She laughed, choking back more tears, so happy she felt like she'd burst. "Okay. Love you!"

"Love you more," Ryan said. "And hurry up, before all these people in my room mother-hen me to death!"

Grinning from ear to ear, Kelsey put the car in drive again and headed for her field office, feeling lighter than she had in years.

"And I want to thank everyone for staying calm and doing your jobs, even during this difficult time," Kelsey said about an hour later. She'd had to call in most of her team and while they weren't happy about it, they'd showed up, which was what mattered. "You're going to hear some shocking rumors and news stories in the coming days about Phil's arrest. If anyone approaches you for comment, please refer them to our PR office. If you have any questions yourself, please know you can come to me. Phil left a stain on our department with his actions, but as long as we remember our motto—justice, integrity, service—we can't go wrong."

As she finished to a round of applause and good wishes, the bell above the door rang and Kelsey glanced up to see Ryan in the back of the office in a wheelchair pushed by Lori, with a smile on his face and "checked out against medical advice" written all over him. His brothers flanked him on either side, looking far less happy.

. . .

Uh-oh.

Her pulse tripped over itself and she finished shaking hands and talking to her team, then made her way back to where the small group waited by the door. Ryan looked pale and exhausted, but he was still grinning, his eyes beaming with pride for her. Her chest squeezed tight as she knelt beside him and took his hands, tears running freely down her cheeks now. "What the hell are you doing here? You should be in the hospital, Ryan."

"That's what we told him," Lance said, scowling. "But he wouldn't listen."

"Said he had to come here and talk to you," Neal added, expression hard. "Idiot."

"Hey," Lori snapped at him. "Leave your brother alone. He was able to convince the doctors to let him leave, with restrictions, so unless your name ends with MD, sweetie, shut up."

Kelsey had never seen Lori and Neal be anything but lovey-dovey with each other, so this was quite a revelation. She glanced back at Ryan, who winked at her.

"Lovers' quarrel," he whispered, loud enough for everyone to hear.

"Shut it, little bro," Neal growled, unamused. "Or I'll take you back to the hospital myself and make sure they keep you a week. Maybe glue your lips shut so you can't sweet-talk anyone into letting you have your way."

Kelsey bit her lip, knowing any threats made were full of love and not menace at all. Ryan rolled his eyes and grinned at her again, still a bit loopy from his meds, she guessed. That was good. The last thing she wanted was for him to be in any more pain. "You should have stayed, though. You've been through so much today, honey. Spend the night in the hospital, let them look after you, take care of you."

He put a finger over her lips to silence her, then traced his finger along her jaw, making her shiver. "The only person I want looking after me right now is you, darling."

Lori set the brakes on his chair, then herded the others over to the opposite corner to give them some privacy. Kelsey said a silent thank-you to her and made a mental note to take her out sometime soon and buy her hopefully one-day sister-in-law the biggest drink of her choosing. Then she turned her attention to Ryan and focused on him alone, the rest of the room falling away.

Ryan took her other hand and squeezed them tight, his own warm and dry. "I'm so proud of you, Kelsey. I know I said that earlier too, but I mean it. I've always held back from commitment, but with you, it's finally exactly what I want."

Her throat constricted and she squeaked out, "It is?"

Blood pounded so loud in her ears she had to strain to hear his response.

"Yes. I want everything with you, Kelsey."

And there went her tears again. Of happiness now, not stress or sorrow or fear. Pure, unadulterated joy. But he'd apologized to her earlier. Time for her to step up and do the same. She inched closer, intertwining their fingers. "You should know that I'm sorry too. For breaking up with you. I shouldn't have done that because the truth is, I want everything with you too, Ryan. More than I've ever wanted anything in my life. And if that means you take this new job because you want it, then I'll adjust as needed. I want you to be happy too, honey."

"I'm not taking it," Ryan said decisively. "I've thought about it a lot and I want to stay here. With you. With my family. Today only solidified that choice for me. I love you and I love the detective work we did on this case. I want to keep doing that—doing work that I love with the people I love." He kissed her hand before continuing. "This case made me remember how much I really dig intellectual puzzles and solving things. I got to do a little bit of that in the SEALs, but not as much as I wanted. There, everything is about following orders. Here, I have the freedom to follow my own instincts and best judgment. Plus," he leaned forward slightly, wincing and lowering his voice, "working with my brothers doesn't suck either. But don't tell them that."

Kelsey giggled through her tears, probably looking a mess and not caring in the slightest.

"Anyway," Ryan said, sitting back again and sighing. "Now that they know about the whole botched mission thing and my discharge, the air is cleared and I know they don't judge me for it. I'm ready to move on, start a new stage in my life, one that includes you, darling, if you'll have me."

"Oh, Ryan." She cupped his cheeks and kissed him, wanting to climb into his lap and cuddle him but knowing that would only hurt him at the moment. So she leaned over the arm of his wheelchair and pressed her forehead against his, never wanting to let him go. "I'll always have you. I love you and just so you know, we are never breaking up again, okay? Even if we don't see eye to eye on things, that's okay. Because at the end of it all, I know you love me and I love you and you accept me for who I am. All of me. And I do the same for you. That's all that matters, really."

They both laughed and kissed, Ryan sliding his hand down her back to nearly grab her butt before she stopped him with a grin. "Hey, I'm still working here."

"Taskmaster," he scolded her in a teasing tone. "Maybe you can take me to task later on in—"

"Uh, Marshal Poppins?" An uncomfortable throat-clearing behind them had her straightening up, face hot and eyes wide.

Oh God.

First night on the job and she was already caught in inappropriate workplace behavior. It didn't help that Ryan just sat there and laughed at her discomfort. Oh, she was going to make him pay for that, just as soon as he'd recovered. Long and slow and hot and deep and…

Get your mind out of the gutter, girl.

She squared her shoulders and flashed her most professional smile, ignoring Ryan playing with the fingers of her hand he still held. He was doing that on purpose, dammit. "What can I do for you, Matt?"

"Uh, since we were all here, we started going over the file on the Jackson case. We have a couple of ideas we'd like to run past you tonight so we can start working on them tomorrow morning, if that's okay?" the young guy said. They'd all come in as they were, so instead of normal suits and ties, some were in jeans or sweats, or even Marshal Smyth here, who was dressed in his favorite sports team's jersey and baggy shorts. Even though it was around thirty outside. Men.

Kelsey sighed and nodded, then glanced at Ryan. "You'll get home okay?"

"Absolutely." He kissed her hand, then tugged her down for another brief kiss on the lips as the others rejoined them from the corner. "We're going back to Dad's house to discuss the agency. Should be fun."

"Tons of fun," Lori winked at her. "Sure you want to miss it?"

"I'm sure." Kelsey leaned down for one more kiss, surprised when Ryan whispered in her ear.

"Darling, as soon as I'm up for it, I'm going to make love to you so good, you won't walk straight for a week."

Flushed and flustered and feeling like she was glowing from the inside out, Kelsey leaned back, trembling slightly again, but for whole different reasons. She gave Lori and the others a shaky smile, trying to hide her aroused embarrassment and failing miserably, if the knowing looks they gave her were any indication. "Uh, yes. Sure," she said to Ryan, trying to keep her cool. "We'll see what the doctor orders, okay?" This time she winked. "You might not have to follow military orders anymore, but this time we're sticking to doctor's orders. For both our sakes. And don't worry. I'm not going anywhere. We don't have to hurry anymore, honey. We have our whole future ahead of us." She said her goodbyes, then turned to Matt, knowing every word she said to Ryan was true. "Now, let's talk about these ideas you and the team came up with…"

EPILOGUE

Eight weeks later…

Ryan sat in a plane at Detroit International Airport, waiting for the pilot to give them the all-clear to exit. He knew most people expected him to be depressed or sad after going through the discharge hearing and formally ending his military career, but honestly, he was excited. He'd already processed all his feelings about that and come to terms with it. And while he missed his SEAL team and would always remember fondly his time with them, he was ready for the future. With Kelsey by his side.

Plus, his SEAL buddies had already set up a messenger chain group that was lighting up his phone like a Christmas tree. Once a SEAL, always a SEAL, they said, and he knew they meant it. He did too.

As the announcement that passengers could unfasten their seatbelts and head toward the exit in an orderly fashion crackled over the plane's PA system, Ryan was up in a flash, grabbing his small carry-on bag from the overhead compartment, then making a beeline for the front of the plane. He'd packed light and felt even lighter, desperate to see the woman he loved after missing her for the week and a half he'd been in DC.

From the way his CO had talked, he'd hoped that it would be open and shut, but with the government involved, nothing was ever so fast and easy. There was a ton of paperwork to complete, then exit interviews and declassification meetings. He'd managed to get through it all faster with the help of his CO, but he imagined someone could get lost in that maze for years.

Now, he was free. Finally free. As he headed down the gangway toward the terminal, Ryan took a deep breath, unable to stop smiling. After all these months of doom and gloom, it finally felt like he was seeing the sunrise. The future ahead of him was not one he ever would have imagined even a year ago, but now he knew it was the right one.

Everything happened for a reason, he believed. It might have taken him some time to figure it out, but he knew he was on the right path now and he was ready for the next chapter in his life. He emerged into the terminal and stood there scanning the area for familiar faces, his new to-do list running through his head. One, tell Kelsey how much he loved her and kiss her silly. Two, talk to his brothers about the Ward Investigation files he'd read on the plane. Three, attend Ruth and Lance's baby shower tonight. Four, wild hot sex with Kelsey afterward. Five, set two alarms for tomorrow morning so he wasn't late for work.

Then he spotted Kelsey in the crowd of well-wishers and he suddenly couldn't wait another second to check off that first item on his to-do list. Maybe check it off a couple of times in a row, just to be extra thorough.

The minute he was clear of other passengers, she was on him. He dropped his bag at his feet and she jumped into his arms, wrapping her arms around his neck and her legs around his waist as she kissed him soft and deep and sweet. By the time she pulled back, they were both breathing hard, and now he was excited in a whole different way. He let her slide down his body, partly to hide his hard cock from the other people streaming around them, but also because it felt so incredible having her close to him again. He locked his hands at the small of her back to keep her there, then smiled down at her like a love-sick dope. Which he was.

"I missed you, darling," he said, staring into her pretty brown eyes.

"I missed you too, honey." She swiped a lock of hair off his forehead, letting her nails gently graze his scalp, and damn if he didn't feel that all the way to his toes. Then her expression changed from playful to serious. "How are you feeling? Leg okay?"

"Leg's fine." He nodded. It still gave him twinges now and then, but the doctor said that was normal and should go away completely in a few months. He was still healing, in more ways than one, but all the signs looked good. "How are things here?"

"Well," she all but quivered in his arms, her eyes bright. "I've got some news."

"You're pregnant," he joked, then wondered if that joke went a little too far. He knew that she didn't see kids in her future, and had already assured her that that was fine by him. She was all he needed—especially since he was going to be Uncle Ryan soon anyway. He liked the idea of having a bunch of nieces and nephews that he could spoil rotten and then pass back to his brothers when they started getting smelly or bratty.

To his relief, she just laughed. "What? No." She smacked his chest playfully, giving him a stern glance. "The regional commander called me this morning and they want to offer me the district director position permanently!"

"Oh, wow! Darling, that's fantastic!" They hugged again, him picking her up and spinning her around while she giggled. By the time he set her down and she stepped away, he wished they could call off the baby shower and head straight home for sex, but no. That wouldn't do. Ruth and Lance would be disappointed, and he didn't want to miss their faces when they opened his gift anyway, so… sex would have to wait a little longer. It had been almost two weeks already. What was a couple more hours, right? Besides, he and Kelsey were sharing hosting duties with Neal and Lori. He'd never hear the end of it from his brother if he shirked his duties, so yeah. Baby shower it was.

The drive to the house was a blur of chatter and hand-holding and kisses. He told Kelsey about the hearing and his time in DC, and she told him about the cases she was working on with her team and the new intern they'd hired after the old one got promoted to full-time administrative assistant in the office.

By the time they reached his dad's old house, Ryan felt like he'd never left. He also felt like he'd come home at last. It was weird and right all at the same time. They got out and walked up to the door hand in hand, but before they went in, Ryan stopped on the porch and turned to face Kelsey, their breaths frosting on the chilly air. "Hey, darling. I love you. You know this is forever with us, right?"

She smiled up at him, then rose on tiptoe to kiss him. "I know. I love you too and always will, Ryan. This is forever."

They kissed once more, deeply this time. Then Ryan opened the door and they entered the house, filled with laughter and love and happy couples all around. Ruth and Lance, Neal and Lori. Ryan and Kelsey. Each of the Ward brothers had found happily ever after, not in the way any of them had planned, but still perfect for them.

He couldn't help thinking that his dad would be proud. Ward Investigation had a bright future ahead of it, sure—but more than that, the Ward family was finally happy.

END OF SEAL'S FAKE RELATIONSHIP
WARD INVESTIGATION BOOK THREE

SEAL's Pretend Girlfriend, March 24, 2022

SEAL's Pregnant Ex-Wife, March 31, 2022

SEAL's Fake Relationship, April 7, 2022

PS: Do you like a man who can take charge? Then keep reading for exclusive extracts from ***His Stubborn Lover*** and ***The SEAL's Convenient Wife.***

THANK YOU!

Thank you so much for purchasing my book. It's hard for me to put into words how much I appreciate my readers. If you enjoyed this book, please remember to leave a review. Reviews are crucial for an author's success and I would greatly appreciate it if you took the time to review the book. I love hearing from you!

You can connect with me on:

goodreads.com/leslienorth

bookbub.com/authors/leslie-north

facebook.com/leslienorthbooks

x.com/leslienorthbook

ABOUT LESLIE

Leslie North is the USA Today Bestselling pen name for a critically-acclaimed author of women's contemporary romance and fiction. The anonymity gives her the perfect opportunity to paint with her full artistic palette, especially in the romance and erotic fantasy genres.

Find your next Leslie North book visit LeslieNorthBooks.com or choose:

BY TROPE

BY HERO

PS: Want sneak peeks, giveaways, ARC offers, fun extras and plenty of pictures of bad boys? Join my Facebook group, Leslie's Lovelies!

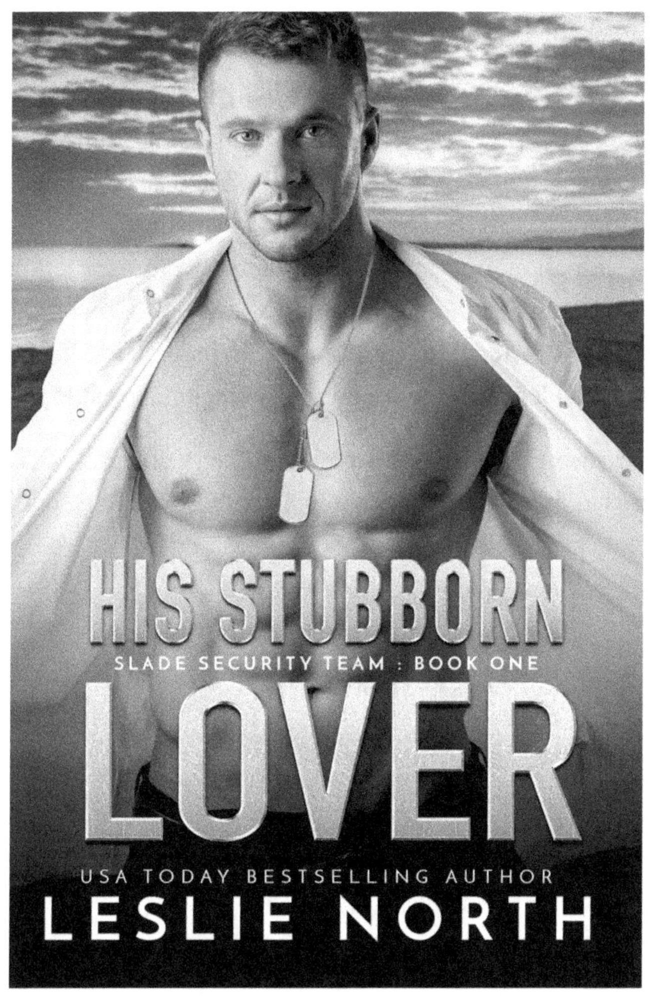

BLURB

Never mix business with pleasure…

Keira Mantz just scored the job of a lifetime. She's been working for a high-end security company for years, and finally she has a mission all her own: to protect Erin, the Sheikh of Jawhara's wife. But what she thought would be a solo operation suddenly becomes a two-person job. And her partner is none other than Brock Wells, the man who recruited her. The last thing Keira wants is Brock stealing her thunder. But she'll do whatever it takes to succeed.

Brock has been avoiding Kiera since the night he found her fighting some very dangerous men in a bar parking lot. The Slade Security "no fraternization" rule is serious business, and with her mile-long legs, fierce determination, and unwavering focus, Keira is a temptation he can't afford. But with the threat to the sheikha closer than they realized, Brock and Kiera have to go deep undercover, posing as a couple. And suddenly that temptation becomes impossible to ignore…

When their ruse gets a little too real, can Keira and Brock risk letting their guards down? Or will giving in to their feelings put innocent lives in danger?

Grab your copy of *His Stubborn Lover*
www.LeslieNorthBooks.com

EXCERPT

Chapter One

5 years ago

Brock Wells exited the bar, heading for his '66 Mustang. The twang of a sad love song followed him out, lamenting the pain of always striking out with women, and his head buzzed with the four beers he'd had. The team had just finished a training operation in South America and Slade had given everyone some much needed time off—meaning Brock had come home hoping to find some female company.

He'd hit a bar that was a ways off from his usual haunts, looking for a stranger with doe eyes and a body that could make him forget just

166

about everything. Tonight, however, his batting average was about as good as the one who wrote that song that he could still hear playing inside.

Well, it was probably better this way. Slade had no rules against team members hooking up outside of the teams, but he also didn't like sending anyone into the thick of things if they had attachments. That was where Brock thrived—in the middle of the worst trouble. This meant that Brock liked his girls for one night only, and every girl in that bar had had the hungry look of a woman hunting a man.

It looked like it was going to be an early night, his favorite video game and a few more beers for him.

Glimpsing movement from the corner of his eye—three figures under the glare of the parking lot lights—Brock stopped, and everything else went into automatic assessment. Some habits never went away, and the ones from his days as a SEAL were deeply ingrained.

Two guys, one woman—and yeah, he wasn't being paid by Slade for this one, but he also wasn't wired to look away. He headed over, took up a spot that gave him the advantage, since it put him right behind the guy holding the knife, and boxed the trio against a battered pickup. He offered a friendly grin. "Looks like a party."

The two guys—good ol' boys by the looks of the wife-beater shirts and sagging jeans, and none too smart to go by the eyes glazed by drink and drugs—glanced at each other. The guy without a knife nodded at the half-empty parking lot. "Get lost."

Brock shrugged to loosen his shoulders. "Let the girl go and I won't have to mess up this crappy spot with your even crappier blood. I'm only asking once."

The girl had guts enough. She kept hold of one guy's wrist—the guy with the knife—but she glanced at Mr. Mouthy and said, her voice low and firm, "Please, I changed my mind, Toad."

"Toad?" Brock laughed. "Seriously, dude? That's your handle? Okay, we're done here." He brought his hand down on the shoulder of the guy with the knife—hard enough for the guy to let out a grunt.

Brock spun him around, punched him once in his soft gut. *Not smart, dude, to let yourself go like that.* The guy doubled over, spilling out whiskey-soaked breath. Brock snapped the knife from the guy's limp hand. It clattered to the asphalt. A jerk back and the guy lay flat on the ground, on his back. Brock kicked the knife away and glanced at Toad —Mr. Mouthy. "You want a go? Your choice."

Before Toad could even bunch a fist, the girl hauled off, caught him in the throat with the flat of her hand, and drove a knee into his groin. The guy doubled over, and Brock gave a sympathetic wince. She kicked up at his jaw with a boot, and Toad crumpled like a wad of toilet paper.

Leaving the two guys on the ground, Brock grabbed the girl's hand. "Come on. Let's go before these two even think about trying a round two, or call for their buddies to come kick our asses."

He pulled her with him, sizing her up as he went. She had long, straight hair, hitting below her shoulders, which looked brown, maybe dark brown in this light. He couldn't judge the color of her eyes, but they were big, dominating a narrow face. Pretty, he'd guess. A little too skinny. A baggy shirt hung down over her hips, hiding anything she might have for breasts, but she had great legs—long and lean and encased in tight jeans. Plus boots made for kicking.

"You okay?" he asked.

She nodded and let go of his hand to go around and get into his convertible. He lifted an eyebrow at that—maybe this kind of gutsiness had gotten her in trouble to start with. She didn't seem to mind jumping into a stranger's car, but then he wouldn't want to hang around either to see how Toad liked being kicked in the nuts.

He started up his car and headed for the highway. "Where do you live?" he asked, leaning over so she could hear him over the wind, which was a soft roar in his ears and a pressure on his cheeks.

She shook her head, captured her flying hair with a hand, and slanted him a look. "No one's ever done that before. No one's ever helped me out."

Brock grinned. "It's kind of what I do." He pulled out a card and slipped it to her. It had his name on it and the words, *Slade Security*. She ran her fingers over the card, and Brock's throat tightened. She had great hands—long fingers, tapering and slim, and strong wrists. He liked the way she moved them, too, slow and certain. They reminded him, somehow, of white butterflies.

She looked at him again. "What kind of security?"

He shrugged. "Whatever anyone needs. Systems. Bodyguards. Surveillance. You name it. Slade Security is a full service operation."

She nodded, shifted so she faced him. "You military?"

"Used to be. Navy. I'm out now." She nodded again and grabbed her flying hair, yanking it back into a pony tail. He put his eyes on the road. He was not going to think about taking her back to his house. Well, okay, he was going to think about it, but he was also going to remember her kicking a guy in the balls. "What about you?" he asked. "Figure out an address where you want me to take you?"

She shook her head. "My cousins set me up to work for Toad. They didn't tell me he wanted to have me selling drugs—and myself."

"Ah," Brock said, and gave a nod. "That accounts for the parking lot disagreement. No folks?"

"Not that I want to see." She faced the road, too. He could tell that from the way the car seat squeaked. "Don't have anything else going for me, either."

He glanced at her again. The light from the dash played over her face. She had brown eyes to match her hair, big eyes in a narrow, heart-shaped face. She'd also held up well in that parking lot, better than most would, and she'd known how to fight. That was a point in her favor. She also wasn't shaking or crying now. He liked that. "Where'd you learn to punch like that?" he asked.

She grinned. "Streets. Where else?"

"The streets. Meaning you fight dirty. That's cool. You want a job?" The words popped out, and Brock wanted to kick himself. That's what happened after four beers—impulse took over and his mouth went on auto-pilot.

He hadn't meant to get into this with her. He'd been taught to protect those around him. The weak. The misfortunate. The ones you loved—those were the rare ones. He thought he'd found that with Tayra. They'd been high school sweethearts and married young, but then the military called and he'd answered and Tayra had left. Since then, he'd always had to watch out for the folks who needed someone, so long as that someone wasn't him. He'd come to hate the idea of meeting his maker on foreign soil and having that tear someone up back home—and it had ended up costing him, since he didn't see any point in getting in a long-term relationship that wouldn't last.

He and Slade were looking to expand the teams with support staff, including getting more females on board. There were some jobs that needed a woman to do things that a guy couldn't, like follow a female suspect or a client into a bathroom. Neither of them was the type to intentionally put women in danger, but the truth was that females could be a great distraction. He glanced at the girl—yeah, he'd bet she'd clean up to be totally distracting.

She hadn't said anything, and he wasn't sure if that was because she hadn't heard him or was thinking things over. He was about ready to write her off—and that was a relief—when she asked, "What's the pay?"

He glanced at her. It was her call to dive into this, and they'd make sure she stayed safe. She'd get training. She'd never go out without back up. That actually might be something this girl could use. If he left her on the streets, there'd be no telling what might become of her. He gave a nod. "Good. Really good."

She stuck out her hand. "I'm Keira Mantz. I don't use drugs and I don't sell them. I'm not up for anything illegal and I have no intention of ever being anyone's property!"

She had enough aggression in her tone that Brock shook his head. But he also grabbed her hand and shook it. She had a firm grip. "Well, don't go all Amazon man-hater on me."

"Why not?"

He glanced at her. Her mouth had twisted into a grimace, and he figured something had put her off men in general. Maybe Toad—or maybe just guys like him. Pity about that, but it'd be better for the job if she wasn't there to snag a guy. "Okay, go ahead with that. I can't guarantee anything, but I can take you to meet Slade. He'll make the final call on you working for us. You want to stop and pick up anything before we head out to meet up with him?"

She shook her head. "I'm more than ready to leave my old life behind. All of it."

Brock put his eyes on the road. He knew about that. Sometimes life just got shitty enough that all you could do was leave the wreckage behind. He pulled out his cell phone to call Slade and set up a meet. The corner of his mouth twitched. Slade was going to love this girl— he just knew it. Brock snuck one more glance at her.

If she was coming on board that put her off-limits. Totally. Pity about that, because Brock wouldn't have minded seeing what she looked like under that big shirt of hers. But work came first. Always. That was one rule Brock was never breaking.

Grab your copy of *His Stubborn Lover*
www.LeslieNorthBooks.com

BLURB

When Navy SEAL Patrick Nelson returns from a black-ops mission, he's in for a shock—his six-year-old daughter Ellery has been abandoned by his ex and is currently in foster care. Now he has to prove he can be a good, stable father to Ellery, and that includes convincing Imogen Mendel, his daughter's gorgeous kindergarten teacher, that he's one of the good guys. Turns out, Imogen is more than just a pretty face. She's planning to testify against some dangerous people who are now threatening to silence her—for good. But not on Patrick's watch. He's got the perfect solution to keep Imogen safe and give Ellery a stable home: get engaged.

Imogen may have agreed to a fake relationship with Patrick, but she has to admit there's absolutely nothing fake about their attraction to one another. It's red hot and impossible to ignore. Before she knows it, they're turning into a real family and her heart is taking a painful turn toward falling in love. Things would be pretty good if not for the threats that escalate as the date of the trial looms closer. Thank goodness she has a sexy SEAL protecting her. But for how long? This fake marriage is turning far too real for both of them…

Grab your copy of *The SEAL's Convenient Wife* (Hartsville's SEAL Heroes Book One) from www.LeslieNorthBooks.com

EXCERPT

Chapter One

Patrick Nelson climbed the steps of the elementary school he'd attended as a kid. The front doors of the yellow brick building stood open to the spring weather, and he frowned. Weren't schools locked down these days? His hand automatically went for a sidearm that wasn't there, and then he gave himself a shake. This was the civilian world, where an unexpected open door meant nothing—and he didn't carry a gun in the civilian world. Well, not usually. And not to pick up his six-year-old daughter.

But he'd been on an extended deployment, and the transition back to life in his hometown was tough… especially since this mission had had more than its share of challenges. Moreover, he felt as if he'd let his responsibilities as a father slip—though not by choice. Yes, he'd been busy and out of touch, but his ex had made things ten times worse. Rachel had completely cut him off from any news of their daughter four months ago. Not one Skype session. No FaceTime. Nothing.

Patrick had been expecting Rachel to be difficult, after the fight they'd had before he left, but this was too much. Their arrangement had to change. He'd taken extended leave from the SEALs, and he was going to fight for full custody. He had no idea what that would look like… but he'd figure it out, because Ellery deserved better.

A man wearing a Hartsville Elementary T-shirt greeted Patrick just inside the front door. "Can I help you?"

"I'm looking for the kindergarten classroom," Patrick said, looking around. The building hadn't changed much since he'd been a student there, but it seemed strangely quiet for a place that housed kids.

"There are three. At the end of this corridor." The man pointed down the hall. "I think Ms. Mendel is the only teacher still here."

"It's only three o'clock," Patrick said with a glance at the oversized clock that hung nearby. "I thought school got out at three."

"Usually, but we had a field day, so the kids went home two hours ago."

Damn. He'd missed Ellery. Patrick had wanted to surprise her by picking her up from school—though he'd been nervous about it, too, since they'd had no recent contact. He didn't know Ellery as well as he should, and even when they'd been in touch, he'd often had no idea what to say to her. Despite that, he'd decided that he wanted to see her without Rachel around to interfere. Maybe the teacher could give him some insight.

"Thanks," he said and made his way toward the classrooms. The first room he looked in was empty, but in the next, a slim woman's figure was outlined against the bright light coming in through a wall of windows. "Ms. Mendel?"

She swung around, her hand going to her heart as if he'd startled her. "Hello," she said breathlessly. "I didn't hear you come in."

Was she the nervous type? That seemed at odds with teaching kindergarteners.

"I'm Ellery Nelson's dad. Is she in your class?"

"Oh, yes, she is," Ms. Mendel said, but her manner stiffened. "I understood that her father was out of the picture."

He held out his hands in a "look at me" gesture. "As you can see, I'm here. Do you need proof?" he asked, taking his military ID from his wallet. He walked closer to her. As he approached and the glare hiding her features receded, he could see she was a young woman with blonde hair. Pretty, very pretty, with delicate features and hazel eyes.

She scrutinized his identification card before handing it back. "Thank you, Mr. Nelson. So, what are you doing here?"

He arched an eyebrow at her. "I'm Ellery's father. I just got back to the States, and I want to see my daughter. I'm sorry you apparently received inaccurate information about my involvement in Ellery's life, but…"

She looked at him a moment and then seemed to relax a bit, though her expression was still guarded. "Why don't you have a seat?"

He looked around at the knee-high chairs and reluctantly folded his tall frame onto one. Maybe she just needed a little more information. "I've been deployed since not long after the school year started," he continued, "so I haven't been here for any events, but I was hoping to pick Ellery up. I didn't realize it was a short day. I guess I'll have to get in touch with her mother," he concluded, trying to keep the frustration from his voice. He wasn't looking forward to having to deal with Rachel, who'd probably do everything in her power to block him from seeing Ellery.

"So you don't know?" Ms. Mendel sat at the desk next to him, looking more sympathetic now.

"Know what?" He felt a prickle at the back of his neck, a sensation he'd learned to heed during his years in the service.

"I probably shouldn't tell you." She paused before seeming to come to a decision and continuing. "It's not really my place… but if I were you, I'd want to know. Ellery's been in foster care for the past two months. Her mother left her with a nanny and then, well, didn't come back. After more than a few days of not being able to reach the parent, the nanny called Child Protective Services."

"What?" Patrick shot to his feet and towered over the teacher. "Child Pro—does that mean foster care? Why didn't someone contact me? Where is she?"

"I can't disclose that." Ms. Mendel rose to her feet and took a step back, crossing her arms in front of her as if to ward him off. Her eyes strayed to her desk, where a phone sat.

"I'm her father," he said through gritted teeth as he searched for the control that had gotten him through so many tough spots. He had no wish to alarm Ms. Mendel. She wasn't the enemy. But she did know where his daughter was.

"I'm not disputing that, but you don't have custodial rights," she said. "You're not even on the list of people permitted to pick Ellery up."

"I'm not?" He and Rachel had talked about that when Ellery started school, and she'd assured him that she'd filled out the paperwork showing him as Ellery's father, with parental rights. Another lie. He shouldn't have been surprised.

"No. Look, I've told you as much as I can. If you want to see Ellery, you'll have to go through CPS. You should go now." Her words weren't an invitation, but a dismissal. He got that he was making her nervous, but he had to ask one more thing.

"Just tell me if she's okay," he said. Foster homes weren't always the best, and he wanted to know that his little girl was safe for now. "Please."

Ms. Mendel's face softened, making her look even younger. "She's struggling with this. Any child would, but I think she'll be okay in the long run. She's a resilient girl."

That helped. A little. But what he'd thought was going to be an unpleasant negotiation with his former girlfriend had just ramped up to a battle with an enemy that he knew little about—with Ellery's safety and happiness at stake. How the hell did he go about extracting his daughter from foster care?

"Thanks. I'll get out of your space now." He stalked to the door and made his way back to his SUV. Just as he was opening the door, his phone rang.

"Hey, man. Got plans tonight?" Anderson, one of his SEAL team members, was on the phone. They'd been buddies since high school.

"I could actually use your help right now, if you're available," Patrick said. Anderson was a strategist and might be a big help in dealing with the bureaucrats at children's services. "Can you meet me at the county office building?"

Anderson's reply was instant. "Of course, but why?"

"I'll explain when I see you." Patrick hung up and drove to the modern building located just outside town. In his head, he replayed the conversation with the teacher. She hadn't shared any information that was helpful beyond that last comment about Ellery's welfare, which he hadn't found all that reassuring. His job was clear, though: he had to get answers and formulate a plan to fix this.

**Grab your copy of *The SEAL's Convenient Wife* (Hartsville's SEAL Heroes Book One) from
www.LeslieNorthBooks.com**

www.ingramcontent.com/pod-product-compliance
Lightning Source LLC
Chambersburg PA
CBHW050515160726
48003CB00001B/310